STREGA

STREGA

Johanne Lykke Holm

TRANSLATED BY SASKIA VOGEL

Riverhead Books
New York
2022

RIVERHEAD BOOKS
An imprint of Penguin Random House LLC
penguinrandomhouse.com

English translation copyright © 2022 by Saskia Vogel
Copyright © 2020 by Johanne Lykke Holm
Originally published in Sweden by Albert Bonniers Forlag, Stockholm, in 2020
First English-language edition simultaneously published in Great Britain by Lolli
Editions, London, and in the United States by Riverhead Books, New York, in 2022

Library of Congress Cataloging-in-Publication Data
Names: Holm, Johanne Lykke, 1987– author. |
Vogel, Saskia, translator.
Title: Strega / Johanne Lykke Holm,
translated by Saskia Vogel.
Other titles: Strega. English
Description: New York : Riverhead Books, 2022
Identifiers: LCCN 2022006560 (print) | LCCN 2022006561 (ebook) |
ISBN 9780593539675 (hardcover) | ISBN 9780593539699 (ebook)
Subjects: LCGFT: Novels.
Classification: LCC PT9877.18.O446 S77 2022 (print) |
LCC PT9877.18.O446 (ebook) | DDC 839.73/8—dc23/eng/20220407
LC record available at https://lccn.loc.gov/2022006560
LC ebook record available at https://lccn.loc.gov/2022006561

Printed in the United States of America
1st Printing

BOOK DESIGN BY LUCIA BERNARD

For Siri A.W.

STREGA

I studied my reflection in the mirror. I recognized the image of a young but fallen woman. I leaned forward and pressed my mouth to it. Fog spread across the glass like condensation in a room where someone has been sleeping deeply, like the dead. Behind me I saw the room reflected. On the bed lay hairpins, sleeping pills, and cotton panties. The sheets were stained with milk and blood. I thought: If someone took a picture of this bed, any decent person would think it was a reproduction of a young girl's murder or an especially brutal kidnapping. I knew a woman's life could at any point be turned into a crime scene. I had yet to understand that I was already living inside the crime scene, that the crime scene was not the bed but the body, that the crime had already taken place.

The bedroom window was open. The air smelled like water, bread, and citrus. I walked over and leaned out. Though the day had only just begun, the streets were steaming with late-summer rain, heat. At the intersection below, the traffic was already dense. Beyond the city, the mountains stood sharp against the sky, which was rumbling. On the horizon lay the large, glittering sea, cargo ships surging and sinking with the waves. The sounds carried far and freely, metallic and dulled. I heard a hammer strike concrete. I heard airplanes in the sky. Down on the square, a ball rolled across the flagstones. I saw a boy in a school uniform set fire to a piece of paper. I saw a girl dragging her dolly behind her. Above me hung the shining sun. I reached for the plane tree growing outside my window. I caught hold of a shoot and stuck it in my mouth. It tasted sweet and rough, like sunbaked resin.

I walked naked through the flat. The living room was all in beige and yellow. A thick dust rose from the wall-to-wall carpet. In the bathroom, the tap was dripping in the dark. I reached for the switch and the strip light crackled overhead. I twisted open the taps and filled the tub, poured in baby oil and bath salts I'd bought with my own money. I lowered myself into the water and leaned my head back. I reached for the hotel brochure, which I kept in the gap between the bathtub and the brown-tiled wall. Each spread showed a slice of life at the hotel. There were high-contrast photos in crisp jewel tones. Girls in pearl-white aprons, girls eating ruby-red apples straight from the tree, girls setting out coral-pink charcuterie on an excursion to a jade-green lake. I had already examined each spread many times. I knew there were tennis courts, a park, a ballroom. Mountains encircling a swimming pool, endless recreational options. I let the brochure sink through the bathwater and come to rest on my stomach, like a shroud. I reached for the shampoo, washed my hair until it squeaked. I scrubbed my cheeks and knees with a brush made of horsehair. I rubbed a small pale blue soap between my hands, and it lathered.

I climbed out of the bath and let the water drip from my body, wound my hair in a terrycloth towel, and walked through the flat, where the air was vibrating. I took out my traveling clothes. A pair of jeans and a shirt I'd stolen. Sneakers made of cotton. I put on jewelry and ran my fingers through my hair, let it rest heavy against my back. I dabbed perfume on the dip of my neck and wrists. I applied lipstick. I sat down at my desk and wrote a farewell note to my parents. Finding the words was easy, because I had repeated them to myself all summer. I pressed my mouth to the paper.

On the windowsill in front of me, books were arranged in symmetrical piles, alongside incense and matches. Opposite, on the other side of the street, was an open window. I saw a child dressing another child. I saw a woman bending over a bed. I saw a man reaching out his hand and grabbing hold. Everything was as it usually was, for now. I reached for the ashtray and lit a cigarette, opened the window, and leaned out. The tar burned in my lungs and spread into my fingertips. If you can't give your body the good stuff, give it the bad stuff. It started raining, the heat eased. I thought for a moment that my hands were giving off the scent of eucalyptus. I stubbed my cigarette out on the window-pane, let the rain wash over my hands for a while.

I folded up the note and walked through the living room for the third time. I always give a thought to when I do something for the third time. I'd advise all people to do the same. It's impor-tant to be suspicious of that sort of repetition. I pinned the note to the noticeboard in the hall and turned in toward the flat, nod-ded to my parents' wedding picture, which was hanging by the hall mirror, and picked up my suitcase, which was sitting by the door. I walked down the stairs and the stairs echoed. I took in the hallway's smell of infants, cigarette smoke, boiled potatoes. I had with me a piece of bread and a pyramid-shaped carton of or-ange juice that I'd put in the freezer overnight. I had with me toiletries and hairbands and notebooks. I had with me a winter coat that I'd inherited. I had with me a silver-inlaid moonstone, which I took to be holy. Once on the street, I turned around and lifted my gaze. For a moment, I thought that my mother was waving from the kitchen window, like something out of a melo-drama. What mother waves to her child from a window. I bit my tongue until it bled. Who are you when you leave your parental home? A young and lonely person en route to life.

The street was slick and smelled of rain, heat. I took it all in. Storing images as if in the face of death. I was a murder victim opening her eyes wide, as though to suck life in. There was the milk bar, where I had worked for many hours, letting my hands stack glasses and cups, wetting my lips with lukewarm milk from the cans. There was the swimming hall, where I had swum my laps. The fountain and the department store. The fruit shop glowing in every color. Ample piles of grapefruit and grapes. Water in plastic drums. The smell of dried figs and wet sand that washed over me as I neared the sea.

)

The station was deserted. People traveled later in the day or not at all. I held my ticket in my hand and the paper disintegrated against my skin. I got on the train. Outside the window, the mountains rose higher and higher and the greenery paled. I traveled through depopulated villages. I read, I wrote postcards, passing orchards, forests, watercourses. A young boy came by with a coffee cart. Chocolate and biscuits were on offer. I reached for a tin of mints but changed my mind. The carriage slowly emptied of people. With every station, someone disappeared. Women in black waved at children in black. A soldier was waving a pennant. People were embracing each other everywhere. In the end, I was there alone.

I rested my forehead against the window and opened my eyes wide. Suddenly everything out there seemed artificial. The mountains appeared to be lit up from below by a bright spotlight. At the foot of the mountain, the trees stood in perfect rows, as though dipped in wax and coated in glitter. On the rhododendrons hung dewdrops of silicone. A roaring waterfall, which seemed frozen in time. I looked at the mountains and the mountains looked back. Without a doubt an evil place in costume. Above the door, a neon sign started blinking—TERMINUS in fluorescent green. I took the pocket mirror from my summer jacket's inside pocket. My face was blank. My mouth was still bright red, but I touched up my lipstick anyway. I put the mirror away and gathered my things.

I stood up and got off the train. Here too the station was deserted. In the transit hall hung a clock. I noticed it was an hour off. The clock struck and a mechanical bird emerged from a hatch, as though guided by an invisible hand. Under the clock was a pool of water, which was expanding. The village was called Strega and it was in the mountains. Later I learned that Strega was a chamber of horrors, where everything had frozen into a beastly shape. I learned that Strega was deep forests bathed in red light. Strega was girls plaiting each other's hair just so. Girls who carried large stones through the mountains. Girls who bent their necks and stood that way. Strega was a lake and the foliage enclosing it. Strega was a night-light illuminating what was ugliest in the world. Strega was a murdered woman and her belongings. Her suitcase, her hair, her little boxes of licorice and chocolate.

)

I walked through the streets. There were no people. There was a post office and a bar, but no vegetables or bread, no living things. On a stone balustrade was a plastic bowl. Steam rose from it, like the steam in a laboratory. I walked on, seeing eyes everywhere. An unsightly child was sitting on some steps and making faces. Drapes welled out of an open window, like ectoplasm. I walked through Strega and arrived at the water, which gave off a familiar smell. Something moldering and somehow tepid, like the night air in a church. On the dock, a semaphore was beating in the wind. From a crevice in the mountains, a ferry came gliding. It was a polished steel vessel with the name *Skipper* hand-lettered in yellow on its side.

I turned my face to the sky. The air tasted like iron, and I licked my lips. Everything was iridescent pink, except for the lake, which was black and gorgeous. The range gleamed and gleamed and the sky was clear. I sat on the ground and lit a cigarette. A young mother and her child were standing nearby. The boy lifted his hand to his face, as though to bat away an insect. The mother grabbed hold of his wrist. I took out the juice carton and drank it down in a single gulp. Then I ate of the stale bread. I tried to find the horizon, but it was hidden behind the mountains. I grew up by the sea, where everything was open planes. I took out my notebook and wrote down my home address, watched my name glow strangely on the page. I had always imagined the future otherwise. I was to work the perfume counter at the department store. I was to save my money and keep it in the bank under my own name. I was to move into a flat where other women were also living, free souls with jobs and love lives. But I did as they had asked of me. I liked being an obedient daughter. It felt like being held by a beautiful patent leather collar.

I let the notebook drop to my lap. The smell of the water was numbing me. I shut my eyes. For a moment the sound of the waves was crystal clear, as though they had washed into my head. Behind my eyelids something surfaced, a sequence from a film I'd seen. A taxi driving through a storm toward a red building. Cobblestones glinting in the rain. In a large hall, patterned textiles hung from the ceiling. A girl walked across the floor with a glass of water in her hand. She had a very anonymous face. Her hair was black and seemed to have been dipped in holy water. I addressed her, but she turned away.

When I opened my eyes, other girls my age were standing around and watching me. I blinked and blinked. The sun disappeared behind a cloud, then reappeared. Around me, the mountains suddenly seemed to rise up like walls. I looked at my hands, which were shaking. With one quick movement, I reached into my pocket and grabbed hold of the moonstone. I gathered my things and stood up. I nodded to the others. They nodded back. We walked to the cable car.

We flew forth above the valley. Motor hammering rhythmically, cables crackling. Around us were mountain clefts, insects, thistles. I looked to the ground, where women were at work. They were wearing cotton gloves and gathering something in large baskets. Wintergreen leaves with sturdy stalks. Autumn nettles, maybe. Mallow. I caught sight of a piece of granite beneath one of the wooden benches. Around me, the others were speaking ceremoniously with each other. They took hold of each other's hands, tossed their long hair and laughed. Next to me sat a girl who seemed familiar. She had one of those faces that could easily serve as a screen for other people's projections.

She said her name: *Cassie*.

I nodded.

I said my name: *Rafaela*.

The cabin rocked and I gasped. We had arrived. One of the girls pulled open the doors, and we climbed out. We looked around. On a tree trunk was a highly polished metal sign bearing the name of the hotel. We started to walk down the only visible road. It was a wide avenue, the forest billowing softly on either side. The road slunk through the landscape and then vanished around a bend. The dust whirled around our shoes. No one said a thing. All that could be heard was the dull, rhythmic crunch of gravel.

As if out of nowhere, the hotel appeared behind a very old oak tree. Right away I noticed that there was something wrong with its proportions. Against the backdrop of nature, the hotel looked like it was in miniature, like a dollhouse that had been handed down through the generations. The facade had at one point been painted a bold red that had faded and was now rather pink. As soon as we were through the gates, they shut behind us. The building sat in the center of a manicured park. There were manicured bushes in even rows. There were whitewashed statues. We walked in a line with our luggage in our hands. The air trembled around us. We passed a fountain and a steaming thicket. There was a smell of dust and water and burned hair. All the windows were open. Music was coming from inside the building. Bright notes pinging the mountains. It was a classical piece that sounded as though it were being performed by an orchestra made up of deeply unhappy people.

I didn't know why the place frightened me. It was a beautiful day, and everything was beautiful wherever I went. I stood still for a moment and tried to fill my lungs with the thin air. The fountain emitted a soft gurgle. I looked around. There was a clothesline and a bed of roses. There was an herb garden. There were wide stone steps leading up to the entrance. The front door was dark brown and seemed to have been cut from a single piece, as from an unnaturally large tree. Someone leaned forward and knocked. I shut my eyes briefly, as though to hide. When I opened my eyes, I was looking right into a grave face. In front of me stood a woman with a duster in her hand. I wanted to laugh but didn't. *You're here*, she said. She was dressed in a black suit, the name Rex embroidered with a silvery thread over her heart. She studied us with half shut eyes before moving aside and letting us in.

We stepped into the dusk. The music was louder here. The floor vibrated beneath our feet. I wanted to cover my ears, rest my forehead against a doorframe, and shut my eyes. The room looked like a scene from some blood-soaked ancient drama, where grave women in draped dresses moved across a stage, knives in their hands. Somewhere on the other side of the set, a chorus shouted its lines about shipwrecks and revenge and murdered daughters. I looked up. Through the dusk, I glimpsed a vivid mural on the ceiling. A stormy sky with scudding clouds, gold accents, and wild horses. All the walls appeared to be red.

The thick curtains were drawn and didn't let in any daylight. The lobby's only illumination was a pair of silver candelabras on marble pedestals set far apart in the room. It could just as well have been a night with a darkening moon. I clasped my hands and looked around.

At the reception desk, a woman was sitting behind a pile of paper. She was wearing a formal suit dress with a figure-hugging jacket. She looked like a secretary. Or rather, she looked like an actress playing a secretary. We were led up to the desk and had to give our full names, so that she could tick us off a typed list. Over her heart was an enamel brooch on which the name Toni was written in italics. She handed each of us a slip of paper with a number on it. The hotel's purple stamp glowed against the white page. I got number seven, which seemed to be a given. When she handed me my paper I happened to curtsy, as if out of old habit. Surprised, she shook her head. She smiled, I blushed.

I ran my hands through my hair and turned around. A woman in a housekeeping uniform came up to me. Her gaze was evasive but friendly. She handed me a basket made from plaited plastic filled with cotton balls and shampoo bottles and hand soaps shaped like fruit. Over her heart I read the name Costas on a handwritten paper tag fixed to her apron with a safety pin.

The moment the last of us had received our slip, the music came to a stop. We gathered in the middle of the room. Rex drew the curtains aside, and golden cascades of afternoon light flooded the room. Under our feet a marbled linoleum floor gleamed. The marble wasn't marble, but hardened oil. Next to me was a bouquet of flowers on a sideboard. Carnations, green, reaching for the ceiling. The vase was knobby and seemed to have been made by a very young child. Clumsy hands that had tried to shape something beautiful. The color reminded me of cough medicine, I could taste it in my mouth. I looked at the other girls. For a moment they all had green eyes. It must have been because of the sudden shift from darkness to light and all the red around us, something to do with the contrasts. We stared at each other, anxious but also smiling. Their irises seemed to be seeping through the whites of their eyes and down their cheeks, only to evaporate there. I lifted my hands to my face. It felt damp.

As if on cue, we cupped our hands over our eyes. We stood like that for a while, breathing deeply. Something seemed to pass through the room. It sounded like a sack being dragged across the floor. We let our hands fall and looked around. The spell was broken. I counted nine pairs of eyes blinking fast, as if in shock. I turned to the mirrored wall on the short end of the lobby. My eyes were black again, as usual.

I broke away from the group and walked alone up the stairs, through crimson and soft-lit corridors, all the way to the seasonal workers' dormitory on the second floor. The beds were lined up in even rows and looked like bunks. On each mattress was a black uniform dress with shiny buttons. It could just as well have been the dormitory of a penal institution. By the window was a bed on which the number seven was painted, white on dark wood. The bed was made with rough sheets. The hotel's emblem was embroidered in purple, surely by hand. I set my suitcase on the floor and went up to the window. Everything was sparkling clean. At first, I thought the windows were glassless. I opened the hasp and leaned out. The air was hot but fresh. I couldn't get enough of that taste of mountain and sun and chlorophyll, my lungs drank and drank. Down in the courtyard, some of the girls had gathered. I think they were smoking under the cover of a bush, or they were discussing something secret, something that demanded seclusion and shade.

Beyond the park, the forest spread. There was no horizon, only a curtain of bark and trunks. Mountains rising to the sky and disappearing among the clouds, which were thin and wispy, as clouds are in the mountains. Autumn was attacking tree after tree. Soon everything would be a flaming yellow. A hot and consuming light would settle upon it all. We were to walk out into the forest. We were to pick berries and make jam. We were to air out our coats in the park. I lifted my gaze. From the treetops an image emerged. As through an oval portal, I saw the contours of a structure. The building was very old, built of roughhewn stones in a simple pattern and surrounded by a small but lush garden. I saw red apples hanging in the trees. I saw bed linens drying on a washing line. I saw that the heat had laid itself upon the herbs and burned them. I thought: A convent. I took out my sunglasses and went back to the others.

We gathered in the staff refectory. They treated us to cherry cordial and almond cookies. We opened wide and swallowed. I felt ashamed of my shoes and my dumb face. I took a seat in the middle of the room, next to a potted golden cane palm. It smelled dry and hot. My shirt gleamed against the Paris-blue glaze. I have always believed this: Hiding is easiest when out in the open, when you unveil yourself as one would a statue in a rural square. Someone whips off a large black velour shroud with one quick gesture. A murmur ripples through the crowd, but no one is looking at the statue. They are all watching a point behind it, something shining in a shop window, a jewel.

At the other end of the room, a group of girls had gathered. They were laughing and touching each other's hair. One of them was talking more than the others. From her hands, a bright light radiated out into the room. I was surprised that I hadn't noticed her until now. She was wearing black velvet trousers and a pale red silk shirt. The shirt was wrinkled and the sleeves rolled up. Her nails were a shrill red, but she had no makeup on and shadows under her eyes, which shone with a deep, magnetic darkness. Her hair was thick, almost black, and disheveled. She had tried to gather it in a large hair clip made of tortoiseshell. I allowed my eyes to rest on her collarbones. There was something soiled but sophisticated about her, and I loved her right from the start.

The hours passed. I sat by my plant, listening and looking. The low evening sun found its way through the open terrace doors, like the glow from the oversize lamp, placed somewhere in the forest beyond the gates. The light beat like a flame against the curtains, which billowed and billowed. I ran my hand over the fabric of my shirt. A smell of sweat and spice came from my armpits. It's humiliating, I thought, to live in this body. Someone ran by in the corridor and I looked to the door. Out of the corner of my eye, I caught a flash of patent leather shoes. No one came. I turned to another girl with a comment, and she responded. Something about parents. Something about sports. A brief and boring exchange. I leaned back. One of the girls walked off and stood by the window. The evening was soft and mild. Seemingly out of nowhere, a hard and beautiful laugh escaped the throat of the girl with no makeup. A confused silence settled over the room before the others finally joined her in laughter, though tentatively. I heard my own mouth give a short laugh as well, before it shut.

The door was flung open, and Rex entered the room with her scent of hair oil and patchouli. She looked at us with disgust, as through a crystal ball that was showing us for who we really were. She took out a cigarette and lit it with a candle. Using the smoke from the cigarette, she wrote "Rex" in the air for us, mirrored and with rounded letters. The name lingered for a moment before it was dissipated and devoured by a gust of wind from outside. She cleared her throat and started reading the hotel rules from a sheet of paper. Her voice roared through the room in a far too steady rhythm, as though the voice came not from a person but a machine. No men in the dormitories or in the staff refectory. No leave, unless in the case of a death in your immediate family. She looked at us: *Dead mothers, dead sisters, that's it.* Everything that happened at the hotel was to be treated as confidential. *We value loyalty here at the Olympic.* All telephone conversations were to go through the permanent staff. *We can facilitate a call home, if need be, but we would rather our girls avoid devoting themselves to homesickness.* Transgressions would result in immediate termination, without pay. *You're seasonal workers, that's just the way it is. Any complaints are to be filed with me personally.* She looked at us, wondering if we had any questions. We shook our heads. Behind me, I heard someone's earrings rustle. Rex lit yet another cigarette, took a deep drag, and stared with measure through the terrace doors. She left the room with a nod, and we breathed out.

I got up and stood next to the girl by the window. The others stayed in their seats, as though paralyzed. I said nothing. I pressed my forehead to the glass. Outside the terrace doors, the park lay in total darkness, but was apparent in its scents. It was a damp night. The dew spread and drowned everything it could reach, intensifying the smell of earth and honey emanating from the plants. The harvest moon appeared in the sky. It was silver and iridescent, like an opal. One wanted to take it in the mouth and place it under the tongue. One wanted to see it spill its milk across the earth, until all was moon. In the middle of the lawn, a red ball lay gleaming. Something glow-in-the-dark in the plastic was making it supernatural. The wall clock in the dining room struck ten. A smell of almond and cherry rose from my hands. A sweeping sound came from the corridor. The woman who was called Costas appeared in the doorway. She fixed her gaze on a point behind us, something she was seeing with her inner eye. She said: *Ten minutes until lights out.* We looked at our hands. Someone whispered something. Someone dropped something. We walked to the dormitories.

I sat with my nightgown in my lap and waited. I didn't want to show my naked self to the others, I don't know why. The moment the electricity was shut off, the dormitory was swallowed by a surging darkness. Everything around us disappeared, but you could sense the park outside the window, you could sense the mountains. I heard someone strike a match against the wall. I inhaled the smell of fire and sulfur. The room was still dark but by the window was a flaming orb, the soft glow of a storm lantern.

The night air in the dormitory felt sticky on my lips. I ran my tongue over my teeth. Overhead, someone was running across the floor. I looked up at the ceiling, where red mold seemed to be spreading in a bad way. Around me, the others were sunken in a communal sleep. I saw their hair sweeping across the pillows, like black shawls. They were sleeping like children, hands clasped, mouths open. On the chairs between our beds, their clothes lay folded in tidy stacks. I looked at the objects that belonged to them. A razor on a nightstand, a bottle of aspirin. Perfumes and matches and sewing kits. I pressed my teeth into my knuckles until my knuckles bled. It seemed impossible to escape this collective burial. I longed for my own room, the locked door, my little cell. I was a lonely person, I had been alone all my life. One is alone even in the company of one's mother. One speaks, and it echoes inside her.

I turned my hands to the ceiling and shut my eyes tight. All my sleepless nights arose in me, as if somebody were emptying something out inside me, a sweet drink with belladonna, as from a pipette. I fell asleep and woke up in the same motion. I opened my eyes and saw a blue haze drift in through the curtains. I recognized the milk of dawn and lifted my hand. I got up and walked barefoot across the floor. I opened a window. Out there, the park lay empty and thick with dew. Everything was fresh, but also seemed old. The harsh light of morning washed over me like grace. The morning air seemed to carry with it a particular dampness, different to any I had known before, as though it had drunk of a holy decoction made from green leaves and wet stones. I leaned out the window, greeted the rhododendrons, the boxwood, the black moss, dug my fingers into the woodbine growing on the facade, let them rest there for a moment, hidden by all the green.

I took great care making my bed, smoothing the cotton with my hands. I went to the bathroom and washed my face with cold water and soap. My eyes burned, and I blinked. The bathroom was decorated like an English garden. Monstrous, artificial plants crawling along the walls and floor. A glassed-in watercolor of a fountain. On the rim of the bathtub sat small bathing beauties made out of porcelain. I hated these porcelain figures, because they represented everything that was wrong in the world. I'd read a pamphlet on Marxism, which I'd been given at the People's House one night, and after that I had cultivated a violent hatred against everything small and everything pleasant. I hated the ornate and the diminutive. I hated dessert spoons and cigarette cases and compact mirrors. I hated my dress and its pleats. I hated sitting on a chair with my legs crossed.

I sighed. Sank to the bathroom floor like a cloth someone had dropped. It's a strange thing to be in the mountains when one wants to be by the sea. I sat like this for a long time, heard the pipes working, heard the water flowing through the building as though to drown it from within. I got up and went back to the dormitory, put on my uniform. It gave off a strange smell of plastic, of industry, which was probably meant to camouflage the uniform's true smell, namely the smell of mold, of some dank basement. I buttoned my jacket and straightened my skirt at the waist. In the mirror, I saw a uniformed and anonymous person, face empty and uninteresting. This was a great relief. I didn't have to show them my true face. It was enough to show them the uniform's face, a face for a decent life, an orderly life. Sometimes I wore my mother's old dresses. I had a red rayon one that made me look like an assistant. I had a dove-blue cotton one that made me look like a government employee. In the uniform, I appeared to be a competent woman. I gave myself a formal nod, gathered my hair in a low bun.

I ran my hand along the wallpaper in the corridor. It was moist like skin and gave off a faint saltwater smell. I opened every door I came to. I found a broom closet, where bottles of cleaning materials stood next to large packs of sponges among messy piles of scouring rags and steel wool. I felt a sudden urge to sort everything by color, fold the rags into perfect squares. The wall-to-wall carpet was like a red river and consumed all sound. At the end of the corridor, hidden behind a thick drapery of imitation velvet, I found a door. Behind it were red-painted stairs. Whirling in the air around me was some sort of powder. There was a scent of moth repellent, slaughterhouse. I couldn't see where the stairs led, but the fear in my chest grew as I considered this red color, like when one walks into a room and is struck by the thought that it is inhabited by evil spirits. On the chairs sit ghosts, drinking water from drinking glasses, opening fruits with their hands. I leaned in so I could look up, but above there was only an opaque penumbra.

The stairs that led down to the lobby were wide and lit up day and night by a row of pink-shimmering lamps shaped like shells. It gave the impression of walking through a bordello, a place where night was eternal and everything took place under the shield of darkness. Unusual scenes in which a girl bends forward in an oversize wedding dress. Unusual scenes in which a grown woman is dressed up as a confirmand. I walked slowly and with control down the stairs, pretending to be making an entrance at a debutante ball, waving with reserve to my many admirers. Behind the reception desk, inside a felt-clad alcove, the room keys hung in a row. Numbers one to seventeen, written in red in roman numerals on oval tags made of dark, thickly lacquered wood. They seemed to be ordered by some incomprehensible system, an order other than that which is given.

I stood and flipped through the register. Empty page upon empty page, not a single guest since the end of June. At the very front of the book, the pages were so dense with names they spilled into the margins. The guests seemed to have come from everywhere. There were names of the rich, but the kind of rich who had inherited their fortunes, as though money were not money but inner organs, something already vested, long before that first morning, that first light, when one, tender and unseeing, met the world. Mothers who birthed blue fetuses with mink stoles around their necks. Fathers who sat fuming on the stone staircase in the garden, after their wife had insulted them by giving birth to a daughter. And everywhere these chambermaids and housekeepers and subjugated women.

I slammed the book shut with a sort of rage. On my hands were marks left by my front teeth. The night's endless grinding. I must have been seven the last time I slept the whole night through, a deep and dreamless sleep free from worry, a small child's corpse tucked into its coffin. I went to the staff refectory. Drank coffee, ate a slice of bread. I held the cup with both hands. It was a porcelain cup with the hotel's emblem. Someone had placed a piece of rock sugar on each saucer. I stuffed the sugar in my mouth and let it melt there. My lips became sticky and tasted sweet. There was a clatter in the corridor outside. Toni, Costas, and Rex had already been working for hours. I had heard them walking across the gravel pitch. I had heard them slamming the doors and throwing the windows open, caught the scent of cigarettes and coffee and newly washed sheets. I stood in the terrace doors and looked out over the park. The ball was no longer glow-in-the-dark, but matte.

The clock struck seven. It was an old grandfather clock with a beautiful tone. I had been sitting by the golden cane palm, watching the minute hand. I had watched thirteen minutes go by. I hadn't blinked. From the corridor I heard light footfalls and bright laughter. I tried to calm my hands, which were shaking. The first person who stepped into the dining room was the girl from the night before, the one without makeup, who was now wearing her uniform, just like everyone else. She looked right at me. Later, she told me that she recognized me at first glance and berated me for not having recognized her. *Life hasn't prepared me for an event such as this,* I said, *of one day running into a person who could reflect one's interior like a mirror.* She came up to me and reached out her hand. It was cool and dry. She said: *Alba.* I replied: *Rafaela.*

She sat down next to me and started peeling an orange. She split it in two and handed me half. She said she came from a town surrounded by fields and plantations. She said it was a humid place, alive and verdant and marked by an unshakable calm. One ate chestnuts, one drank white wine. I looked at her, bewildered to hear someone speaking directly to me for the first time in a very long time. In my mouth, the bitter sweetness of the orange. She looked encouragingly at me, asked where I came from. I heard myself talk about the ocean and the cargo ships. I said: *One eats bread, one drinks spirits.* She nodded. Around us the others sat scattered, draped over armchairs or leaning against the walls, they were smoking and laughing and drinking sugared coffee. Everyone had their uniform on. Under the scent of dry shampoo and cheap perfume was the smell of mold, which was our sign. It was as if I could suddenly reach for the other girls through Alba, as if they had been standing there waiting for me the whole time. They were nineteen years old, just like us. They came from large cities and small villages. They had no money. They had parents, they had no parents. They leaned against each other. It was not simple and lighthearted, as I'd thought. It was necessary. We were here together, belonged together in this way. I looked at our shoes, which conformed to the feet, part of the uniform, which made us look like nurses in some psychiatric clinic, during an eternal night shift with the strip lights blinking harshly in the corridors.

Alba sat and pointed next to me. *Gaia*, she said. This was a thin girl with large hands. She was smoking at the terrace door. Her boyish face was beautiful beneath her short fringe. She looked like a soldier from the infantry. I blushed. *Barbara.* A very athletic girl, her hair loose over her back. She had a rosary in her hand, fingers running across the beads, she was counting. Alba said: *Cassie, a nickname for Cassiopeia, a name that she apparently hates with a passion.* This was the girl I had spoken with on the cable car the day before. One didn't need to look at her for long to understand that what was common about her face was a mask. Beneath it was a serious person with impassioned eyes. Her plait reached all the way down to the small of her back. Alba pointed: *Alexa.* A lanky girl with thick socks. I recognized myself in her. I could see that she and I were daughters of the same industrious order. On the floor, a girl sat cross-legged. *Bambi.* She was a strong person with distinct features. Her eyebrows were thick lines. It was clear that her parents hadn't been able to predict this young woman when they christened her. I pictured her baby face. The baptismal font and the christening robe and the smell of carbon. A priest who said: *Bambi.* In the window sat a red-haired girl peeling an orange with a small knife. Alba said: *Paula.* She looked like something out of a film, something unearthly. On her wrists, she wore bracelets with various charms made of colored glass. Blue and green shapes that clinked as she moved her hands. She lifted her gaze and looked right at me. I looked back, as if through an archway with perfumed water trickling from the ceiling. Next to her sat a girl with chestnut brown hair cut into an impossible style. I saw her soft essence. Something purple and smooth that one wanted to press to one's chest. I saw her run her hand over the wallpaper, just as I had done. Alba said: *Lorca.* I nodded.

I turned to Alba and said: *Have you known them long?* She talked about them as if they had all grown up together, as if they'd walked along the same mountain walls on their way to a rural school, as if they had whispered together behind the shed at the back, as if they had loved each other like brothers. And she raised her eyebrows and replied: *I don't know them.* I said: *You speak of them like one speaks of brothers.* She smiled. Shut her eyes and leaned her head back, against the wallpaper that gave off a thin steam, something pink that came out of the walls and wafted toward the ceiling. *I speak of them like brothers because we're going to need to live like brothers.*

All day we walked beside each other, while Rex showed us the hotel's various facilities. She pointed at the swimming pool and said, in English: *Swimming pool.* She pointed at the mangle and said: *Laundry press.* She let us feel the quality of the towels. She let us run our hands over the kitchen counters. She let us stuff lemon balm in our mouths. I plucked up the courage to lean against Alba. Her clothing smelled of rain. I inhaled her scent and shut my eyes. When we walked down the stairs to look at the wine cellar, I let my hand graze her uniform. She took my hand, as though by mistake, but held on to it. During question time in the ballroom, I wrote a few words down and gave them to her. She read the note and folded it up, then stored it in her breast pocket.

We were nine young women doing seasonal work in the mountains, or nine young women put in safekeeping on the backside of the mountain, or nine young women who watched their hands being put to work, watched them lift starched fabrics to their face only to let them fall to the ground, watched them pour strong wine out of large carafes, like the hands of a statue, right into the parched earth, as though to sate it. We came from various places, but were of the same age and mind. None of us wanted to become a housekeeper, and none of us wanted to become a wife. We had been sent here to earn our keep, to become people of society. We were daughters of hardworking mothers and invisible fathers who slunk along the walls. We were in the mountains because someone had sold something. It could have been silver, it could have been heirloom gems. It cost money to send your daughters to the mountains. Daughters needed tickets, visas, milk chocolate. Daughters needed amulets. This could be a gold-mounted box inlaid with clear plastic stones, where she, the daughter, could store the only treasure she had ever saved: a milk tooth on which the blood remained.

Our parents were all deluded about the fact that the world had changed and would not go back to being what it once was. They did not believe in a future without the good woman and her duties. They wanted to prepare us for a life where we would care for child and home, where we would stay with one man, no matter who he was, where our hands would repeat the same movements. At the hotel, our hands always repeated the same movements, but this was no place for good women. Our parents had imagined the hotel to exist in another era, that it was in fact possible to send us there, to a place where no time had passed, as if we could slip behind a curtain, where the evil steam of reality could not reach us.

The hotel, which was in an isolated valley, surrounded by black mountains reaching out of dark and humid vegetation, by a small blue lake with icy water, had once been a famous and much-frequented place, a place for wedding parties and winter sports, a place that seemed magnetic, where it lay sparkling red among all the green. No one remembered when the hotel had begun to change, when the place had begun to seem repulsive to all healthy people, as though it possessed an inherent power, something fiendish and sick that kept people away. A suspicion was that a poisonous plant had begun to grow many years before, a plant that was now in full bloom. Someone had planted rosary pea. Someone had planted henbane. There were rumors that it was the nuns. The convent had been where it was for all of human time. The nuns had walked the same paths, drawn water from the same streams, dressed in the same starched cotton. They had lived this life, dipped in formalin and embalmed in the face of eternity, right up until the day the hotel was built.

The conflict between the nuns and the hotel staff was deep but unarticulated. One had never spoken ill of the other. One had never taken action. One had seen the other, one had nodded. The hotel had appeared one summer, as if out of nowhere, like something demonic. Demonic, not because of the sin inhabiting it (women in pink furs, men with large hands, small bottles of strong drinks), but because of the way it situated itself in nature, like a piece of meat, a primal cut, something animal and dripping. The nuns spoke of the hotel in hushed voices. They never used its real name, they never said: *Hotel Olympic*. They said: *Il Rosso*. It was said that they walked by with bowed heads and rosaries in their hands. They prayed, they counted. It was said that they suffered and that one left them to their suffering. This happened many years ago.

It was a different time when we lived there. The hotel was

no longer demonic, but had instead become a relic from a long-buried era. One might imagine a hotel as a lively place. One might imagine clatter in the kitchen and clinking glasses, the smell of lilies and something metallic, a tray set with cups and coffee. One might imagine a hotel as a place for people, but that wasn't the Olympic. At the Olympic, the clatter and smells were enclosed in the walls, like a haunting or a flickering memory. Everything was built on a grand scale. The ballroom was enormous and the suites facing the park seemed endless. One could stand at either end and call out to each other, as from a mountaintop. In the kitchen were three long and wide workbenches, where it was clear that there had once been intense activity. One could picture it. Old-fashioned food laid out on white tablecloths. Pineapple ice cream and oxtail soup. Vile things to stuff in the mouth.

It happened that I leaned against one of the large industrial cabinets, chewing on a carrot. I could conjure up whole scenes in the room before me. Large platters of meat and vegetables. People in white shouting to each other. Pretty girls on the waitstaff. Behind this hologram was the reality, a hotel business in utter decay. In one corner, Costas was cutting celery into small cubes. Alba stood next to her, blanching tomatoes. It was all very dull and unglamorous. Scenes from a monotonous and unbearable life. The gray light fell across Alba's face, as if to insult it.

Johanne Lykke Holm

It happened that I walked through the woods to consider the hotel from a distance. I looked out over the bitter waters of the Alpine lake. On the other side, the hotel rose out of the forest, red and immovable, a monument to long-dead maids and their shrouded knowledge.

)

There came a day when we were to go out to the park and harvest the fruit before it fell to the ground and spoiled. There were
apple trees and plum trees, cherries and mirabelles. We lifted our
hands and lowered them. We had baskets and knives. I knelt by
the rose-hip bush, running my hands over the plump, flame-
colored fruits. A red mist hovered above the lawn. I sat within it
and inhaled the red.

There came a day when we were to make dumplings. We
filled them with dark berries. We filled them with meat. We
lowered them into boiling water. Watched them sink to the bottom only to come rushing back to the surface, like drowning
schoolboys full of desperation. The perforated ladle scooped them
up and rescued them to a hand-painted plate of thick porcelain.
A complicated pattern of roses and insects. I imagined the hand
that had painted the plate. Thin and bony and with red-painted
nails.

There came a day when we were to learn the forms of address in various languages. We said: *Mademoiselle.* We said: *Gnädige Frau.* If we met a child in the corridor, we were to tilt our heads and ask: *Where is the young gentleman's mother?*

There came a day when we were to iron, mangle, and fold. The room was filled with a hazy light. Wetted sheets in swelling piles. We had placed the ironing boards in a row. In the window was a black porcelain vase, out of which a lone sunflower was drooping. Rex handed out wrinkled linen. We were given small glass bottles of water with which to wet the fabric. The irons crackled. The air in the room grew hot and sort of aromatic, as if someone had lit a scented votive candle. I lifted my hands and lowered them. The hands knew all about this work. Starched fabrics to bring to the face. Pale pink, steaming.

There came a day when Costas taught us all about lactic acid. We cut cabbage heads in half and picked at them with our hands. We were to pluck out the cabbage leaves in as pristine a state as possible. It was a strange plant. It looked fake, unnatural. Like something that couldn't possibly have come from the earth, something made up, the product of a peculiar thought. The leaves came in all different shapes. Light green ovals. Kidney-shaped leaves with a bright sheen. I held a leaf up to my mouth. The coolth of crops. The moisture they bear: the memory of the earth and darkness, wetness.

There came a day when Toni spoke for two hours on the topic

of *Woman's Plight*. We found it hard not to laugh. There was something touching but also very ridiculous about this woman, who seemed to come from another time. She spoke of men and their desires. She spoke of women's lack of the same. She said: *One stands in the kitchen fixing the potatoes. The telephone rings, it's him. One's heart is pounding in the chest. One goes to the little mirror in the hall. One wants to apply eyeliner, but must give up, for one's hand is shaking too much.* A woman's happiness is serving a man potatoes. One wants to sit upon an upholstered chair, legs crossed. One wants to place one's hands in one's lap and let them lie. I leaned against Alba and pressed my mouth to her neck.

There came a day when we were to learn about the convent. We read about the nuns and their palladia, their holy books. If we met them by the lake, we were to be polite but distant. We were to bow our head to our chest and mumble a brief greeting. We were not to enter into conversation. We understood that the nuns' life held a certain power of attraction. We understood the great risk it would imply if we happened to get too close. Perhaps we would be drawn into their magnetic field and forced to stay there forever. We knew that they lived out their youth outside of youth. Beyond the time of female friends, forever in the time of nuns. They hid their hands in cotton gloves. They arranged mortar in particular patterns. They had long conversations about herbs and saints. There were no mirrors in the convent, but one could use a glass shard, the backside of a spoon. They sanctified the carnation because of its preternatural ability to survive. The nuns studied death as they did any other subject. Toni said: *They do not work for the living, but for the dead.*

There came a day when Rex told us about the electricity, the disciplined force. She wanted to show us the difference between artificial and natural light. She held a light bulb in one hand and a candle in the other. In the light of the bulb, she looked like a lit-up tombstone. In the other, she looked like an actress, soft and veiled in mist. She fixed her eyes on us. She said: *Never switch on the electric light in the dining room without my permission.* I looked at Rex, and she looked at me. She held up the candle in front of her. Her hard face in the warm light.

There came a day when we were to stand with our backs to the wall and perform a series of uncomfortable movements.

The days passed, no guests arrived.

We quickly learned that each day was a reproduction of the last. Morning after morning, we set out coffee and bread in the conservatory facing the park. There were large porcelain bowls filled with black marmalade. There was silverware on linen napkins. Morning after morning, a metallic light fell through the room like a butcher's knife. I stood and watched it happen. At the same moment, Alba walked through the room with a large platter on which fake fruit was glistening. The others folded napkins, set out drinking glasses, topped up sugar bowls. I stared into the park. For a moment I thought I saw someone coming, but I must have been mistaken. I went back to work. Refilled the coffeepots, sliced the tin loaf. No guests arrived.

We made the beds on the first and second floors. We laid out small blue and pink soaps. We smoothed our hands over the decorative pillows and aired the bedcovers. We gathered the hotel's every fabric and washed them. We washed the silk sheets from the suite by hand in brackish water and hung them up to dry in the park. We ironed them on a low temperature, we did not mangle them. We wore gloves. We sprayed orange-blossom water. We boiled the cotton sheets, then ran them through the mangle while they were still damp.

We stood in a row along the kitchen worktops. Costas let us whip cream, she let us proof dough, she let us wash thin porcelain in large tubs. Alba loved being in the kitchen. This surprised no one. She could carve vegetables into beautiful flowers with the help of a paring knife. From a block of cold butter she could make a pale yellow rose. She'd wear a hairnet, so no one would have to find a long hair in her legume salad. The knife she stored in her back pocket, wrapped in a handkerchief. It happened that she took it out and held the tip to my chest.

With Costas, we were happy for brief moments of time. When she wanted to, she could be a rest home, a palm grove. She would put out edible herbs in low glass vases. A great armful of sage that gave off a greenish purple dust. Bishop's-weed and red clover, a bowl of dried nettles. Everywhere, the good smell of coffee and cherry compote. She gave us food to eat. In this way, she was a mother. We were given bread and oil and tins of pickled fish. She gave us milk to drink, because she had a notion that it would make us round and strong and spare us from all that was evil. She gave us generous breaks. We walked slowly through the park, we smoked. We rubbed each other's hands with arnica salve. Alba and I stood for a while, staring out into the forest, where a thick mist came rolling from the moss. We said nothing, we smoked. When the break was over, a little bell rang in the kitchen. It was a beautiful sound that rose into the sky.

The afternoons belonged to Rex. These were the day's most difficult hours, not because the work was hard, but because she was both unreliable and a disciplinarian. She watched our hands as we set the table in the dining room for the evening. We set out ashtrays and drove in the drinks trolley. We arranged the flowers harmoniously on the tables. We fixed our faces in front of the mirrored wall in the lobby. We set out meat and vegetables and crème caramel on glass platters. Rex observed us. I looked at her. She leaned on the mantelpiece, where a violet glowed in a vase made of silver. She looked like a person who had been alone since birth. The clock struck seven. No guests arrived.

Two hours later, the dinner service concluded. We stood in a row in the dining room in our aprons. At a silent signal from Costas, we began to put everything back on the serving trolleys. We rolled them into the dumbwaiter. Staring down at the tainted meat as the waiter sank toward the basement floor. A slice of lemon had slipped off the platter and landed on Alba's shoe. I had the urge to put it in my mouth but didn't. In the kitchen, the fridge was humming. We switched on the light and saw how everything was bathed in the same cold light. Through the airing window, which was open, the metallic smell of wet earth could well in from the park. Someone turned on the radio. The late broadcast from Tirana was on, with dance music and world news. We wrapped the food in aluminum foil, put the wine bottles back in the cupboard. We sat down on the kitchen floor and stretched out our legs. Lorca made coffee in her special way. We drank it with sugar, we smoked. Bambi wiped off her lipstick with the back of her hand and yawned. Outside, the park was silent. I leaned my head on Alba's shoulder. Breathed in her scent of rain and sweat. The break lasted for thirty minutes.

For the rest of the evening, we kept to the ballroom, where the walls were covered with mirror shards arranged in a kaleidoscopic pattern. An electric chandelier bathed us in its hysteric shine. Toni instructed us in conversation and rhythmics. She said: *It's important that a woman be competent, but she must also be spiritual.* She had us line up. She had us lift our feet in one synchronized movement. She had us pronounce vowels as softly as possible. She had us laugh like women. We were to be beautiful children with the proficiencies of adults. We were exhausted and moved through the room like rag dolls. She handed out liqueur and herbal candies from the convent to keep us awake. The room steamed with the sweet scent of malt syrup and thyme. One stretched out a foot, one bent forward. One imagined a businessman's face and his smile upon seeing us come walking through the lobby.

Only at midnight did we fall into our beds. In spite of the

rain, the nights were still hot and dense, they quivered. The moon was up, I saw her through the curtain. I sat in bed and studied my face in my pocket mirror. The night air wafted around me with its sweet scent. I noticed that one of my eyes was glistening in an unsettling way, as though black obsidian had moved into the socket and replaced the eyeball. The others fell asleep in the blink of an eye, facedown, like corpses in a very old funeral rite. Their hair welled across the sheets like spilled ink. When night reached its deepest point, I fell asleep too, submerged in their sleep. We all dreamed the same dream. It was a walk on the beach in summer. We came walking together. The sun, white, vibrating above us.

)

On a shelf next to the bathroom window, with a view of the herb garden's unruly and dark green vegetation, Costas had collected all the books left behind by hotel guests over the years. There were crime novels with glossy, lurid covers, pictures of naked women with open mouths, large hands reaching for their tools, a noose or a knife, something very small that resembled a poison ampoule. There were disintegrating cream editions, slim books of poetry that someone had tried to mend with glue, a teenage boy's sensitive hands, the smell of turpentine. There were luxurious volumes wrapped in tissue paper, carefully packaged but never read, green leather bindings that gave off an oily scent.

We stood and chose together. We watched the greenery reach for the building in desperation, as if it knew that it would soon wither and perish, along with all else that was alive. We wagged our feet, ran our fingers over the book spines, turned our heads to read the titles. Lorca pulled out a book from the row, said: *This one*. It was a hard book with a baby-blue cover. The title was in large, rounded letters: *Marienberg*. The outline of a rosary was embossed on the spine. We nodded and Lorca pressed the book to her chest, as if she feared someone might steal it, snatch it from her hands in an unexpected movement.

We had started reading aloud to each other the very first week. Sundays, the day of rest, spread out like a vast field, so we read to pass the time. Sitting together on the sofa group in the lobby, handing out candy and cigarettes, leaning against each other and closing our eyes. During those days, the lobby floor slowly filled with porcelain bowls and platters and big jugs. Black porcelain, red porcelain, hand-painted porcelain with pictures of caddis flies and Hymenoptera, a child's hand holding a rattle. Bowls of dried fennel, mint, and saffron. Bowls of brutti-boni and bomboloni. We drank barbajada. We drank black coffee. We drank vodka that someone kept in a flask. Sometimes we read the whole night through, until the ghost-dawn rose over the mountains. Sometimes we fell asleep and woke up again in the same motion. We lit candles and fetched the storm lamp. Now and then, Rex would walk through the room, and everything hushed. She looked at us, but said nothing.

I stared at the book in Lorca's hands. In my mouth I could taste its color. Bambi said: *Comrades*. And we walked toward the kitchen, where everything smelled of metal and water and heeled-in crops. We filled a plastic tray with biscuits and jasmine tea. Alba pinched the liqueur from Costas's supply. We carried everything up to the lobby and settled into the white leather sofas. It was decided that I would be the one to read. I had a penchant for making words rise from the pages like black smoke. I could raise and lower my voice with conviction. I could shout like a grown man and cry like a girl in the same breath.

Marienberg began with a young and lonely person walking through the mountains. It was a beautiful night, and she took on its beauty. Something flashed, and she looked. It was a piece of silver jewelry that someone had dropped and then let lie. A charm bracelet. She picked it up and laid it in the palm of her hand. Immediately recognized it from her mother's jewelry box. She put it in her pocket and walked on, as if through a bad dream. Everywhere, the inexplicable smell of death and celebration. As the sun rose over the mountains, she arrived at a convent, where she was welcomed like a lost son. The abbess showed her the kitchen, the well, the herb garden. The little convent, located amid rueful solitude, surrounded by drought and lashed by storms, was made up of thirteen identical cells. The sisters devoted themselves to manual labor and prayer. The abbess looked at her, and she nodded. A shovel was put in her hands, and she began to dig. It looked like a child's grave, but she kept digging. Dusk fell, and the scents arrived. Before her the convent sat in blue darkness. The ivy harried in the garden. There were moss phlox and violets. The climbing hydrangea crept toward the cypress, which looked out over a sea of Breckland thyme. She saw the ivy reaching up and disappearing over the roof. She dug and dug. Evensong echoed against the stone walls. The contractions came along with the night. She stood with the shovel in her hands. Her body was a universe. Her body was a ceremonial tool. Everything was taken apart and put back together again. The pain came from a place beyond everything. She opened her mouth and tasted the liquid dripping from the moon. The liquid that flowed from the tap in the sacristy. It tasted of gold flake and green vitriol. It tasted of formaldehyde. Afterward, everything was dark joy. The smell of blood and milk and rain-soaked earth. She nursed the baby, who was the most beautiful of all children. She wrapped it in cotton and laid it in the garden, among herbs and flowers, together with a handwritten note to the abbess. She clasped the silver jewelry around the baby's wrist, said a short prayer, and disappeared back up the mountains.

I fell silent and let the book sink into my lap. Around me, the others were sleeping. It was night and the moon hung heavy over the mountains. I set the book aside. Out in the park, a girl seemed to be patrolling. I heard her footsteps on the gravel but couldn't see anyone when I looked out.

We sat on the gravel with our backs to the fountain. We leaned against each other, we smoked. I looked at Alba. She had cut her hand. Her thumb was wrapped in cotton and jutted straight out. I leaned back and closed my eyes. From behind my eyelids came a flash. It felt like being inside a blush-red insect with an armored shield. I opened my eyes. Paula said: *I got a letter from my boyfriend. Suddenly, he seems so infinitely boring.* We laughed dryly, we smoked. Somebody offered around sweets from home. We ate them with our hands, passed around boxes in various pastel colors printed with rippling rivers and dewy roses. Our hands carried a sweet scent with them into the evening. Dates and mints. Almonds rolled in pink sugar. Cut marmalade. The fountain's lapping and our voices. I leaned against Alba. She placed a hand on my forehead, said, *Rafa.*

Gaia looked up from the book she was reading: *What did Venus actually do with the unicorn?* Above us, the sky turned cobalt blue and menacing. Paula turned around and blew smoke in my face. I smiled. The day was hot, and thunder loomed overhead. I looked at the hotel. The windows were open on every floor. A potted plant had fallen from the windowsill and landed in the flower bed. Tobacco plants and cacti stood in a row in the late summer light. Clothing hung on the clothesline. Black cotton dresses and nightgowns. Underwear dried in the sun out back. One never knew when male guests might arrive. Doctors, fathers, or priests.

I turned my gaze to the dormitory. Three almost square windows with sparkling glass, reflecting the surrounding Virginia creeper. For a moment, it was as if I could see my own face on the other side, a motionless phantom, forehead pressed to the glass. Her face was identical to mine, and she was wearing a dress I recognized. I usually sat on windowsills, because there was always a chance one might fall out. I sat there at dawn and in the witching hour. I sat there as night came creeping with its evil face. I turned to Alba and pointed, said: *Look.* She opened her eyes wide and nodded.

It was night, and the terrace doors were open. We lay close together on the parquet floor of the ballroom. We had slipped out
as soon as the others fell asleep. We had cigarettes with us. We
had lit incense and candles. The flames multiplied in the mirror-
clad walls. Above us hung the crystal chandelier, swaying slowly
in the breeze. Everything glittered darkly. I had a taste in my
mouth like blood and cream. Alba was as quiet as a stone, but
warm and soft and wide awake. We saw the night being poured
over the mountains as if from an invisible pitcher. I stretched my
legs to the ceiling, let them drain of blood. I said her name. She
stretched her legs to the ceiling, let them drain of blood.

I said: *Where I come from, there is no childhood. I know that there*
was something wrong with me at the time. It happened that I kneeled
on the floor by my bed. It happened that I tilted my head back and let
my chin fall. A blue light streamed through the window and I opened
my mouth to drink. I walked around the apartment wanting to

destroy myself. Searched the drawers for dangerous things. I liked melting candle wax and dripping it on my hands. I liked fire and knives. I liked the smell of petrol. I gave myself new names and wrote them down. I was a strange person. I was melancholic and passive, brutal and entertaining. I had an unpleasant but infectious laugh. I had friends, I hated them. I had parents. I don't know what to say about my parents. They had friends, they hated them. We lived to-gether in a very small space. We always had. We walked past each other, we slunk along the walls. Our apartment was a tinned scene. A diorama submerged in hot formalin. Nothing ever seemed to happen in there. We looked at each other, we nodded. Nothing happened.

Alba shut her eyes, she said: *Where I come from there is no youth. One grows up right away. I had left school nine months earlier. I had looked like an overgrown confirmand in my graduation dress. I had lifted my hand and waved. I was alone, but surrounded by peo-ple. I was to do something with my life, but I had the urge not to. I had books to read. I had hair to tend to. I had my grades and my graduation gifts. I had set them out in my room. Nickel earrings and gift cards. A telephone made of Bakelite. A portable file for my im-portant papers. From my parents, I had received a medallion with a lock of my baby hair. Small palladia for my childhood and my future. I had just learned to smoke. I had a soft packet that I carried with me. In my older sister's eyes, I could see a paralyzing fear that came from what they already knew, that I couldn't yet know. Inside me still sprouted a dangerous mix of optimism and an appetite for destruction.*

I felt like a sequoia drawing poisonous water from the earth. I felt like a mannequin leaning against the wall of an illuminated shop window. I felt hermetically sealed, but was therefore also invincible.

I took her hand: *I waited and waited and nothing happened. I lay on the sofa in my nightgown. I lay on the bed in my gymnastics costume. I lay naked on the floor and breathed deeply. I waited for my body, which was growing. I waited for my brain, which had always been the same, but which lived a secret and eclipsed life. I waited for my inner self to show itself to the people around me. I waited for triumphs and renown, statues of plaster or marble, my portrait in a corridor of some institution or agency. I would look down at the passersby, and they would see me. A line of children would walk by with pennants in their hands. I would own things: metal objects and fabrics. I would be a hand that waves from a car polished to a shine. Beyond the window lay the city, trembling in the light. It's a port town. One knows it by its name and by its scents. There is a body of salt water, there's willful plant life climbing over the stone walls, there are long, wide streets stretching out and up from the sea. I lived there, among the cargo ships and the bars, in the scent of tar and motor oil, and I grew and grew, in step with the palm trees along the boardwalk, in step with the black mold, in step with all the other young women on that side of the mountains.*

Alba said: *What I do with my hands has never been important to me. There is nothing that interests me less. Let them dig in the earth. Let them brush against each other. Let them arrange silly little things by size. But the hands' lack of freedom is also, it turned out, the prison of the soul. I decided to let the events of my life find me and not the other way around.*

I turned my gaze to the door, where a shadow flitted by, said: *Inside the diorama was an ongoing struggle that seemed never to end. It was important to my parents that I enter the workforce, that I reach out into society, that I become a person of use. The first time I worked with something other than my embroidery, I was thirteen years old. They sent me to pick bay leaves in an ochre-yellow and secluded place, where the plant dust fell from the trees like rain. The plantation seemed endless, and I walked through it with my hands turned to the sky. My neck was scorched by the sun, and my feet calloused like the feet of a grown man. It was a fantastic time in every way. When I turned fifteen, I got a job in the milk bar around the corner. I ran down the stairs in my pink uniform. I poured milk into tall glasses. I served cold soup. I knew where the vodka was stashed and which regulars gave the best tips.*

Alba turned her head and looked at me: *Across the street from my sister's apartment is some student housing. I used to hang out there, by the main entrance, staring at anyone who walked by. They were all carrying bundles of books and wearing those sand-colored wool sweaters, you know, the ones one imagines smell like horsehair or a rug ruined by damp. When I saw them, I wanted to spit, but I didn't, out of self-respect.*

I nodded, said: *From my seat on the living room floor, I could see my mother walk by. She had cut out an ad from the newspaper. She called to me, as if I were on the other side of a frozen lake: A hotel in the mountains is looking for nine maids for the winter season. I replied: What's wrong with the milk bar. She looked across the room at me. In her eyes, I could see something taking shape. I shut my eyes, I waited. I heard her sending for brochures. I shut my eyes and waited. Under my mother's supervision, I sent off a thick envelope marked "Olympic," in which a handwritten letter of recommendation from the manager of the milk bar was folded together with a school photograph of my face, a list of my measurements, my weight, my shoe size. A letter in which I detailed my hobbies. Reading, sewing, alpine activities. Well, you know. I held the envelope in my hands and let it fall. I waited.*

The night air streamed in from the terrace doors and over us. Alba sighed: *It was the same for me. It had been raining for weeks. Down on the street, transparent pale blue umbrellas passed by, transparent raincoats in green and yellow. There were alternating downpours and lulls, a strange rhythm that seemed eternal. The city was drenched and had taken on new forms. The concrete changed color, turned dark blue, turned purple, before finally fading in the sun, evergreen and dusty. The vegetation sweated and sweated, cooled down greedily when the rain arrived. I saw that the sea lavender and twinspur had begun to grow unchecked. The eucalyptus tree beneath my bedroom window seemed grotesque. I could reach it if I stretched out an arm. I had seen the notice on a lamppost on my way to work. Nine hotel maids for the winter season. I told my mother. She didn't look up, but said, You're looking. I watched my hands send off an application, as easy as nothing. I saw it happen and thought that something in me already knew that I was on my way out. Away from the sisters and the girls' bedroom and the slow demise. Away from the rain and the damp-stain and all those bad people and their bad lives. That night I bathed my face in Vichy water, slathered myself with cold cream, poured oil in my hair, and shaved my legs. I wanted to get my body in order, for the first time, to prepare it for what was to come.*

I turned on my side, looked into her eyes: *I saw the sun rise and fall over the rooftops. I ate what they put in front of me. I chewed on a cherry pit for hours, until it was silky and smooth and started to taste bitter. I sat in a window and closed the curtains. I heard them looking for me. I heard them calling my name. I didn't answer, but reached out a hand through the gap in the curtain. One day, a few weeks later, a letter arrived in the post. It arrived along with that strange spring, the hot wind that found its way in everywhere. The letter was written on thick yellow paper and had an oily stamp. We have the pleasure to inform, I read, and drew a breath. Something sank inside me and kept sinking. My mouth went dry, and my tongue stiffened. I lay down on the floor and stayed down. I was a sanatorium patient sunk in an induced sleep. I was an embalmed corpse. I let them step over me. It was their punishment, their cross to bear. All of June, I wore my father's shirts. All of July, I painted my nails lemon yellow. I cut a fringe, in August, with my mother's nail scissors. And all the while, my departure lay on the horizon like a threat, a blue smoke spreading.*

And Alba: *When I think that we could have gone a lifetime without meeting, I get a sinking feeling, something at once frightful and exhilarating. Imagine, what a sad life. Then one might as well have been born a stone. A volcanic stone that closes in on itself, as in death.*

And me: *When I think that we could have gone a lifetime without meeting, I would rather die. I'd rather be a beautiful corpse than live one second without this. I walked through the city, where everything was steaming with late summer rain, heat. I arrived in Strega. Everything seemed impossible around me. And then you arrived.*

She reached out a hand and stroked my cheek, said:

And then I arrived.

Of Strega, we knew a series of things. It was a village in the mountains. There was a black lake served by a ferry. There was a paralyzing silence. We knew one could get there by train, as we had done, from one of the towns on the other side of the mountain, on the coast or on the moors, towns with parks and public baths and nightclubs, port towns where cargo ships beat an uneven rhythm against the quay. One could come walking from the mountains in a winter coat, as if one had lived up there in voluntary isolation, as if one were a nun. The lake was beautiful but deceptive. A shiny mirror that reaped several victims each year because of its strangely powerful currents. The village was so high above sea level that it seemed one could in fact reach out and touch the sky. One flew forth above the valley in the cable car. One extended one's hands toward the sun, eyes shut.

In a brochure, one could read about how the nuns produced a bright green liqueur that tasted of plant and sugar. There was an

advertisement printed on glossy paper, in which a nun was rais-
ing a glass to the sun. One drank the liqueur as if it were holy. It
was tapped into large bottles and sold in the villages. Large
boxes were packed under cover of darkness and sent to the sea.
We imagined them holding out their hands in the light and
something rising from their palms, the smell of syrup and preserved fruit, the smell of infants, the smell of skin that had long
lain in water. We saw the boxes being unloaded at the kitchen
entrances of restaurants and bars, nightclubs and cafés. We saw
people by the sea drinking of this sweetness. We saw them form
their mouths into round holes, dip the tips of their pink tongues
into the green liquid, like kittens. From the chestnuts that fell
from the trees in the cloister garth, they made a thick puree,
which they poured into aluminum tins on which a shiny chestnut gleamed against a bright blue background. They manufac-
tured candied chestnuts, which they divided among mint green
boxes. One fed them to each other, straight from the hand.

In an illuminated shop window on the main street were a
series of objects that testified to the fact that Strega once had
been a place of ore mines and gemstone experts. Rock crystals
and amethysts were lined up on a cloth of dark blue velvet, which
gave the lilac stones a ghostly glow. Lavender milk spilled across
a night sky. Postcards of photographs of miners with great ham-
mers slung over their shoulders. Postcards of mountains stretching to the sky, colorized a sunny hue, because the true light of

the sky had a brutality to it that had no place on a postcard. On a shelf behind the counter were long rows of souvenirs. One could buy a miniature mountain church. Baby cutlery shaped like mining tools. One could buy a snow globe in which the hotel glowed red against a green backdrop, as in its heyday.

We were visitors to Strega and could never be anything else. We held porcelain in our hands. We held leather in our hands. We stood on a summit and looked out. Glistening church spires in the morning light. We saw monuments hidden in dark greenery. We saw children on their way to dance class. We had a camera. We always photographed the same thing: silver objects in the sunshine. The sound of someone's voice in Strega. The smell of her hair. Eerie plants and fruits, edible things, a palm branch in the snow. Figs and capers in our hands. Golden tangerines in our hands. We were to wear black dresses and gloves. We were to touch things and say, *Oh!* We were to walk through the days, and the days were to walk through us. We were to extend our hands to the sky and stand that way.

They wished us ill, and they wished us well. No person is ever just one thing. I remember Rex's hands and her eyes. I remember Costas, who always seemed to be filled with a great physical reluctance when she was to discipline us. Toni, who, like all the soft people of the world, was a passionate sadist.

It happened that we were made to line up in the corridor. They asked us to get down on our knees, and we did as they asked. They swept something across our backs. It might have been a steel comb or a scrubbing brush. It never occurred to anyone to turn around and look. They inspected our hairstyles, sniffed our necks, buttoned buttons, and sprayed us with rose water. They hit the soles of our feet with the unknown object.

It happened that Toni thought we were too fat and refused us food. We came down to breakfast, and the tables were empty. Sometimes they had set out strong tea and hard-boiled eggs. Sometimes they had set out nine glasses next to a carafe of water and a jar of dieting powder. Sometimes we had to go down to the root cellar and bring up a vegetable ruined by the damp. I stashed a box of chocolates under the bed for these occasions. Asked the others to open wide, so I could feed them liqueur-filled chocolate and French nougat. It happened that we were to be punished for some transgression. Foul language. Long baths. Nightly absences. All punishment in the hotel was collective. They treated us as one body, so we became one body. We forgot our individual traits and our individual responsibilities. If one of us stole a coin, all of us had stolen a coin. They poured boiling water over our feet and made us dip them in tubs of ice. The pain was unbearable, but no marks were left.

In the place where the forest merged with the park, where the jasmine met the moss, lay the herb garden. It was arranged around the foundation of a long-demolished house, where we pretended that once there had lived a very old woman, who watered the earth outside her window each morning with a special decoction, a magical water that smelled of dead lilies and looked just like melted silver. We saw her pouring out large jugs made of black porcelain. We saw her hands reach for the earth and grab at a gleaming flower. We saw black forest berries and ivy, her dark infusions, her plant dyes. When we worked in the herb garden, we pretended that she was still there as a ghost, and we poured out tea and cordial on the earth, as if to honor her memory.

I stood and watched the others as they worked among the herbs. Their cheeks glowed in the dawning. Their shoes were clunky, clogs or rubber boots. They wore gloves and sunshades.

They took small breaks, plucking refreshments from a basket by the foundation. The sun emerged from the fire that surrounded it. I plucked a plum from my apron pocket and stuffed it in my mouth. The taste spread from mouth to heart and to my chest. Earth and purple sugar.

I sat down on the ground and ran my hand through the plantings. It was a thoroughly beautiful place, and we considered it holy from first glance. The ivy climbed over the wet stones, up to the fence, where it wound itself around the iron bars like long fingers. In one single chaos we grew rosemary, sage, parsley, catmint, marjoram, thyme, herb of grace, bay laurel, dill, oregano, aloe, arnica, basil, summer savory, tarragon, lemon verbena, chamomile, red raripila mint, hibiscus. These were the good herbs one could take in the mouth. One could lie in the shade, lavender melting on the tongue. One could kneel and run fingers through the red raripila mint. One could lie down in the tillage, as if on a bed of herbs, face to the ground.

On the other side of the building, where there was no shade and the sun shone the strongest, was the evil tillage. We discovered it one morning as we were picking weeds along the fence. Someone suddenly pricked themselves on something, and we looked up. There it was, the death tillage. Even rows of wicked herbs, drinking and drinking of the broiling sun. We saw the whiteness running through them like poison. Oleander, belladonna, tobacco, and rosary pea. One could gather up a full arsenal of poison in that garden, feed someone the white sap from a small spoon made of gold.

I drove my hand into the wet earth. Heard the nuns walking through the forest. And I saw them, walking slowly across the moss. The mountains had always been theirs. They knew the powerful grace to be found in herbs, plants, rocks. The abbess took up the lead. I heard her call out: *Good spirits are drawn to the scent of sweet perfume, holy water, salt. Evil spirits are drawn to the smoke of henbane.* She stopped, and said: *Sisters, there is an impression in the ground shaped like a female body. Look! A red smoke is rising from the hole and spreading.*

)

In the early morning, I dreamed that we went on an outing to a place called Èze. I had never been to the place and knew nothing about it. We walked hand in hand through a cactus garden. We saw a panoramic view. We drove along the coastal road at high speed. Through the window of the tourist bus, we saw milk thistle, roses. We held souvenirs in our hands. Around us, grown women were gossiping. Over the loudspeaker someone said: *Please consider that there are innocent children around.*

When I woke up, a memory came to me, as if it had forced itself out of the dream. I was contemplating a statue of the Madonna in an ornate country church. She was beautiful and soft, grace radiated from her hands, but her eyes were dead. Tears spilled from the corners of her eyes, a yellowish liquid running down her cheeks. I reached out and pressed a finger to her face. Stuck the finger in my mouth. Something sweet and bitter that put my tongue to sleep.

I said to the others: *I had the strangest dream.*

Paula replied: *So did I!*

And Cassie: *A dream in which I pricked my finger on a human-size cactus.*

And Barbara: *In which I saw the sea stretching toward the horizon like a beautiful carpet.*

And Alba: *In which I held a crucifix and marzipan sweets and snow globes in my hands.*

I got up and walked through the room. It wasn't the first time our brains had flowed from the same source. I looked at the foliage through the dormitory window. Autumn had arrived overnight, as if on command. Down in the garden was a wet and untouched earth. The trees had let go of their fruits and allowed them to fall to the ground. Perfect gleaming shapes in the low grass. The air smelled familiar and overwhelming. Roses stood in a vase on the windowsill beside me. They too appeared to have been struck by the autumn. Their color seemed deeper now, softer. I reached out my hand and took a rose petal in my mouth.

Lorca wrote down the information from the dream in a notebook, which we kept in the sock drawer along with a little silver bell and a few bottles of essential oil. The notebook was filled with a long list of similar events. The time we dreamed about the men in the church. The time we dreamed about the water cistern. The time we woke up suddenly with the same movement.

Bambi said: *It's autumn.* I nodded and ran my hand across her cheek. Everyone looked mournful, but no one knew why. We hung our blankets out the bedroom window and let them soak up the cold air. From the suitcases under our beds, we took woolen coats and scarves. We put on sailor sweaters. We wrapped ourselves up in shawls. We let our sunglasses sit in our hair like jewelry. We went into the park, where the air was clear and sweet and saturated with scent. Black spot disease had harried among the roses. We picked off the blighted and fallen leaves and placed them in an enamel pot, in order to burn them. We looked for milk thistle but found none. The dream hung in the air overhead, pulsating. All day we repeated the same word: *Èze, Èze, Èze.* We looked at each other and laughed. It didn't mean anything.

We gathered by the fountain. We leaned against the balustrade, turned our faces to the autumn sun and shut our eyes. The mountain mist, which throughout the night had lain thick over the park, had lightened and left behind a heavy and somehow ancient damp. The sheets on the washing line looked transparent, as if they were made of silk organza. From the fountain rose the scent of fresh water and wet rock. I smelled my hands. Earth and sweat and moldering plums. I took Alba's hand and she smiled, eyes shut as if in sleep. From the hotel we could hear the vacuum along with something else that sounded like a hammer.

Rex came out of the lobby dressed as a forester. She had left her hair unoiled, and big, soft curls framed her forehead. She was dazzling, and resembled a beautiful prince I had seen once in a magazine. She noticed me observing her. My cheeks flamed, and I turned away. She called out: *Let's go.* We followed her across the gravel, through the gates, and into the woods. We walked for a long time. The vegetation shifted color from light to dark, as if the forest were emptying of chlorophyll the deeper in we went. I saw plants that made me think of the city park back home. I recognized the heather and the boxwood. The violets that had sunk toward the earth. We were silent, strode through the forest like tough angels. We only stopped once the trees were all black and the moss dark and shimmering. We fell to our knees by a gigantic tree bearing red fruit. We stuck our hands in the earth. We were to study the plants and their ranges of application. Chew leaves and spit them out. Gather berries and cones in a basket.

Costas had sent us off with parcels of food, which we had picked up in the kitchen. We spread out some blankets and set up. We poured bitter tea from a large thermos. We brought the cups to our mouths and drank. Chests rising and falling. There was a heat in the stomach that spread to the fingers. We handed around thick slices of bread wrapped in greaseproof paper. We lay looking up at the sky, which was visible between the treetops. Rex sat leaning against a tree, smoking slowly. I kept glancing at her. The sky laid itself over me like a horse blanket. I shut my eyes.

There was a rustling somewhere behind us and I opened my eyes. A little ways off, a nun walked by. She walked down the path with a basket on her arm overflowing with some sort of woodland herb, bright green. She walked bent over. Her dress snagged on all sorts of things: rocks, thorns, and bushes. In her hand she held a twig, thick with red flowers, branching and spreading out. Red flashed at her feet. For a moment I thought she was wearing patent leather shoes. She was the incarnation of a nanny in a movie I'd seen. There was something serious and industrious about her forehead. Cassie cried out: *Hello.* Rex shot her a terrified look. The nun did not return the greeting, just carried on.

I sat on the floor of room seven with my back against the wall. Beside me, a newspaper from the year I was born. There was a whole double-page spread about a family found dead wearing their formal clothes. In the nursery, the children were tucked with their christening spoons in hand. In the next room, the parents were slumped over the dining room table set for a feast, sitting on either side of a brief letter, which the newspaper had printed in its entirety as a photocopy. Their signatures were shaky, but the letter was hardly sentimental.

I had just vacuumed the wall-to-wall carpet. Motes of dust still hung in the air around me, along with the smell of electricity and lavender. I had set out fresh flowers on the bedside tables. They smelled strong and alive. I preferred things that were dead to begin with. Marble and metal things, things of hardened plastic. I stretched out my feet and let them rest. I inspected the room. Everything was purple in there. The polyester curtains and the carpeting, the wallpaper with the small floral pattern. In the bathroom there was a tap that only dispensed scalding-hot lilac-colored water. Just looking at the water one caught its smell. One imagined a day in May. One walked between the buildings, which were glittering.

I had begun to suspect that certain rooms I cleaned had never been used. The rooms stood empty, but the beds were always made. This was my work, to prepare for these nights that never happened. I called them the ghost rooms, not because they were haunted, but because rooms unvisited by humans simply begin to attract evil. The rooms had in common that they carried an unpleasant odor that seemed to have no source. It smelled of raw meat and red mold, as if the rooms were spoiling from the inside, as if they were soaking up tainted lake water from some hidden place under the building. And now this piece of evidence, the newspaper, which had lain in wait for me under the mattress topper like a strange gift. I folded it up and tucked it under my apron. I ran my thumb over the mirror glass next to the double bed. It left a greasy mark, but I let it be.

The days passed, no guests arrived.

The theater was in the mountains, situated on a ledge overlooking Strega, which stretched out beneath us, gleaming silently. Toni had decided that we were to be rewarded for our hard work. *Something spiritual for the girls*, she had said with a smirk, her mouth painted a shade of orange that made her cheeks glow like plump citrus fruits. We had opened our eyes wide, we had nodded.

We were each given a ticket and our own box of dark green throat pastilles. The auditorium smelled strongly of smoke and soft soap. I was sweating. In a silver vase on the floor was a large bouquet of carnations wrapped in cellophane. To my hands, the velvet seats felt like fur. It went dark around us, and a black-haired actress, younger than us, made her entrance in a jester's costume adorned with little bells and large beads that looked plastic. She wore yellow shoes and yellow socks and silk ribbons around her wrists. She moved across the stage like a panther or a child phantom, materializing for a second behind a decorative pillar then vanishing, as if in one and the same movement, only to suddenly come crawling out from a velvet cloth that had been discarded on the stage floor.

There was a scene in which her murderer bent over her with an open mouth. There was a scene in which he grabbed her by the throat like it was nothing. I stared at him and saw that he was beautiful. He had a wicked face with soft features. One wanted to turn away, but couldn't. One wanted to lie with him in a grove and rest. One wanted to give him things. Soaps, gloves. One wanted to be something to him. Water over his hands, red light through gauzy curtains. The actress wrenched herself free from his grasp and walked up to the raised seating. She was not afraid. She said: Isn't that the divan on which your father bled to death? He looked at her from across the stage. It was a disciplinary but also gluttonous look, which made me queasy. He walked over and lifted her up, slung her over his shoulder like a sack filled with something heavy. He looked to the audience and smiled, as one smiles at an accomplice. He lay the girl down in the middle of the floor. Her face was like a mask. Mouth red and alive. Various extras came onstage. The murderer seemed to be in control of everything. The game was to walk up to her with various tools. The game was to do things to her body. Someone picked up a rose and handed it to her. She shut her eyes. Someone walked up to her and sliced the skin across her chest.

Someone leaned in and licked up the blood. She looked out over the audience and said: *This is the story of a teenage girl's longing for violence and humiliation.* Her hands moved in beautiful patterns in front of her face. One saw her back. Her face was turned to the white wall, hands raised in a V. She slid down the wall, leaving behind her traces of red, a sign of blood. I looked away and took Alba's hand, staring at the scallop pattern in the decor to avoid seeing what came next.

Did you see him, she said during intermission, *the murderer's face.* I shrugged and bowed my head to hide my blush. *I had an urge to put a curse on him or stab him with my knife.* She laughed. Something dangerous coursed through me, a poison disguised as nectar, which my body was unsuspectingly gulping down. I pulled Alba close, to avoid myself. We walked together to a concession in the wall, where an old woman was selling red and yellow soft drinks in glass bottles. *One yellow,* Alba said. *One red,* I said. The drink tasted chemical and made my teeth ache.

The foyer looked like the waiting room of some government institution, where evil was upheld and distributed in a steady, daily rhythm. There was no marble and no gold leaf, no purple velvet draped from the ceilings. We sat down on a hard laminate bench and waited. Over in the corner, Cassie was making a selection at a vending machine. Black-and-orange packets of chocolates and caramels. Something that looked like powder.

After twenty minutes, a bell rang and we went back to the

auditorium. The poison in me had spread to my hands, which were sweating. I sank into the chair and leaned on Alba's shoulder. The rest of the performance was no more than a bloodbath. Young boys poured a viscous red liquid from large containers made of light blue plastic. Shouting in the wings, a chorus of women. I shut and shut my eyes and only opened them once the applause was ringing through the room like the birth of a child.

Outside the theater, after the performance ended, Toni said: *Girls, it has been decided that you are to be given overnight leave. Go out and amuse yourselves.* We looked at each other, smiles dumb and triumphant. We took the cable car down to Strega, which was glittering beautifully at the foot of the mountain. At the station building, we found an inn, right next to a machine that sold chocolates, cigarettes, condoms. Above the door dangled a wood carving of a nun and her tankard of beer. We went in. At each table were small packages wrapped in tissue paper and tied with string. I leaned over and picked one up. Inside the packet: sweets and herbs. I stuffed a leaf in my mouth. It tasted strong and perfumed, caused a thick fog to settle over my brain. My tongue doubled in size and fell asleep.

The bartender looked at us. In his eyes we could read something like writing. We ordered nine glasses of clear spirits and offered them around. We smoked and drank. We took each other's hands in the middle of the table. We licked our fingers and pressed them to the tissue paper. Alba said: *It does something to the head, one goes light and heavy, one can enter the brain as if it were a hallway in which someone has set up various objects, porcelain things, metal things, golden velvet fabrics that fall from the ceiling like a curtain.* The bartender smiled at us, and we shut our eyes. The evening seemed endless. We drank and drank and got sick from the spirits. We were the only guests. We looked at each other: exhausted faces staring hollow-eyed. We rested our foreheads on the table for a while. Time passed. We half slept in the soft silence, in which a clock seemed to be ticking behind thick drapes.

I opened my eyes. The bartender was gone. Alexa sat next to me, smoking. She looked like an icon painting, her face radiating as if it bore a holy light, mouth forming a circle, the symbol of eternity. Over her shoulders, a ruffled shawl. Smoke rose from her hair like a halo. Her irises ran through her eyes and down her cheeks. I looked down at myself. There were stains everywhere, and my skin was like that of a corpse. I was disgusted by the nicotine yellow glow of my hands. I met Alexa's eye. She smiled and said: *Rafa, shall we go home so you can sleep?* I nodded and leaned on her. The room seemed to grow and shrink around us. The ceiling lowered and lowered, until it was one with the floor. We woke the others. I gathered the remaining herb packets and took Alba by the arm. We fell out of the fog and turned to the sky. We inhaled the fresh night air, drank it greedily like water from a tap. We stood with our hands turned upward. The mountains emerged from the darkness like great pillars. Alba bent over and vomited. I stroked her hair, and she laughed. It was a dry laugh that made something inside me melt.

The last cable car had gone. Someone shouted *Taxi!* and it echoed in the mountains. We giggled and started walking. Past bald parlor palms and rock crystals. The dawn arrived as we walked. The smell of sage, milk, resin. A cold light rose from the forest around us. The light came from below, as if it were the ground and not the sun that was shining. For a moment, we were part of a different order, outside the true order, where the earth radiated and the sky spread out above us like a mute, light-reflecting material. I was cold and pressed myself to Alba. She seemed perfectly clearheaded, as if her body had rid itself of an unnecessary burden, and so her thoughts had free rein. She talked loudly about all sorts of things, and I walked beside her, dizzy and strangely light, like the lone survivor of a mining accident.

We had hidden in the conference room to avoid Rex. On the ceiling, a fan was whirring far too quickly. No one had held a conference in there for many years. Still, a smell sat on the beige-painted walls, of smoke and dust and bad men's cologne. Today the smell was thick around us, as if there were in fact a little gentleman having a cigarette somewhere, sheltered in the half-light. Textiles hung over the backs of the chairs, and the curtains were drawn. Everyone was scattered about. Flung across the office chairs like sleepy children. If I bent down, I could see Lorca on the carpeting under the table. She was stretched out on the floor with a handkerchief over her face. A kind of meditative practice, which she believed could cleanse the soul of all the ugliness it had soaked up in the night.

Alba sat at the conference table eating preserved chestnuts from a tin on which the nuns' emblem glowed green against the bright metal. Behind her, a window was open. I saw that the sun hung heavy over the mountains. Sunday had sunk down on the Olympic and settled. Everything seemed struck by cold, everything was steaming. I sighed loudly and let my hands fall into my lap. I felt ugly and like a failure. Tried to understand how I was supposed to endure this long life, where one was to arrange oneself into a woman each morning. Where one was to wash with a coarse sponge dipped in boiling water. Where one was to rinse one's hair in apple cider and let it sparkle in the sun. Where one was to bathe one's face in brackish water. Where one was to keep cold cream on the nightstand. Where one was to have baby hands with painted nails. I looked at my hands. Like the hands of a murdered woman. I brought my hands to my face and caught a whiff of liqueur and tar.

In the mountains, the men drove by on their motorcycles. Behind the curtains, the noise grew stronger then softer then stronger again. They came from Strega, and they were ascending. The bright burn of their headlights swept through the room. Figures appeared on the walls, oval shapes that waxed and waned, something that was lit up in a flash. White light through the curtains, the smell of petrol and burned rubber. I had a notion that the men were going to come to us. I had a notion about what would then happen, just as all women have this notion, always, that it's only a matter of time. I used to sit in the window and scout. One caught sight of them walking through the woods, so one crouched down. Hunters and tourists with cigarettes in the corners of their mouths. Brutal hands gripping very small objects. Outside the window, the noise grew stronger then softer then stronger again. We heard a motorcycle braking at the gates. We looked at each other. A worrying silence, followed by light footsteps across the gravel. We heard him whisper something, before he started the engine and drove away.

The Virginia creeper turned red one day at the end of October. We woke up and saw a red glow outside the dormitory window, leaned out and caught sight of all the red, the greenery transformed. Later that same morning, as the autumn sun streamed through the terrace doors like a fire, Rex said: *Tonight is the night.* We looked at her. *Guests will be arriving.* We opened our eyes wide and straightened up. She continued: *Cassie will perform her dance.* All eyes turned to Cassie. She blushed behind her fringe, which hung down her forehead like a thick curtain. Rex snapped her fingers, we looked at her. *The rest of you will assist us with the preparations. You are to pick something up in Strega.* In her hands she held a pile of papers, which she asked us to pass around. Instructions and lists and tasks.

It turned out that, in the mountains, a holiday was celebrated which we knew nothing about. For everyone who lived in this place, it was a holy day. One gathered autumn leaves and twigs and burned them in piles. One cleared the land ahead of winter, celebrated the winter. In the evening, one drank spirits and ate small dumplings. Boys in papier-mâché masks appeared in the kitchen windows. One carried pumpkins and sang. It was a festival of death, like the backside of the vernal equinox, a worship of the world's every grave and sinkhole and poisonous plant.

Every year, the Olympic organized a function to mark the festivities. People came from Strega and the surrounding mountain villages. At midnight, a show was held in the ballroom, which we found out would be lavishly decorated with torches and fruit and paper decorations, in which the hotel's most talented seasonal staff were made to move beautifully across a temporary stage, a platform made of straw and cardboard that someone had painted in bright colors.

It turned out that Cassie had been made to rehearse more than once, not knowing for what she was preparing, while the rest of us cleaned and chopped and mangled as usual. This came as no surprise to us. Her body knew more about dance than anything else. As soon as Rex had left the room, we gathered around her. She said that she'd been made to stretch her toes and turn her hands to the ceiling. She said that the managers had dressed differently than usual. She said that they appeared to be floating through the room in their floor-length dresses and soft cloth shoes. She said that Toni had played the piano while Costas shouted incomprehensible things, such as: *Be blue smoke rising from a lively river.* Or: *Be sowbread growing from snow-covered earth.* She said that Rex sat in a corner watching her, in anticipation of her own entrance. It was she who played the part of the lover.

The rule was as follows: Cassie would dance, and she would be a hit. The rest of us would stand along the walls and cheer. The salvos of applause would ring out and shouts of *Bravo* would ring out and the guests, in that electric atmosphere, would declare that the Olympic was still alive, that it was a tremendous place, that the girls at the Olympic were like no other girls.

I walked slowly up the stairs to the managers' quarters, through the corridor, where black carpeting swallowed all light. The walls were pink, and from the ceiling hung fluorescent tubes that looked like they came from some long-shuttered factory. It was my first time there, normally we weren't granted access. All day, we'd been gathered around practicalities. Biscuits to be baked and cloth to be ironed. We'd hung a sign over the ballroom door. *Ballhaus Olympic,* written in yellow on glossy paper. We'd hung cellophane and silver lamé drapes. We'd hung green and pink lanterns. We'd laid out small napkins with ribbed edges. We'd set out bouquets of dried roses in shiny metal vases. We'd set out the incense and matches. We'd aired our clothes, we'd washed our hair. We did all this in silence. We only looked at each other, said not a word about this strange performance in which we partook, clueless as to the role we were in fact expected to play.

The air in the staff quarters was thicker than in the rest of the hotel. It was like breathing the air in a room where someone had switched on a smoke machine. I heard water rushing through the pipes somewhere at the end of the corridor and went there. It was a white-tiled room, the size of a feed hall or an autopsy room. The three women were lined up in front of the mirror in identical black crushed-velvet dresses. They dipped their fingers in a jar of some ochre-red color that emanated a strong smell of earth and water. I thought: red clay. I thought: Where did they get that from? I watched as they pressed their hands to their mouths. A beautiful shade that made their eyes glow. I positioned myself in the doorway. I said: *Let's go.* They nodded. I said: *Let's hurry back.* They looked in the mirror, they nodded. I saw Toni lean forward and smear the red color on her cheeks. It was her signature. Rex stood up straight and poured oil in her hair from a bottle made of smoked glass, in which a thick liquid moved slowly, like dark syrup. Costas looked at me through the mirror. She smiled, though behind the smile lay something poisonous, spreading its green light. She said: *Have fun.* Rex gave a laugh. She turned to me, and I met her gaze.

I walked back through the corridor. Below me was the black river. Everywhere a scent of silver polish and lavender. I walked quickly down the stairs, all the way down to the others, who had gathered in the lobby. Bambi was leaning against the reception desk. On the stairs, Gaia sat tying her shoes. Alexa was smoking with her forehead on the window glass. The cigarette smoke swept across the glass in great swirls, then floated toward the ceiling, where the ceiling mural as always radiated blue and pink. The others stood in the middle of the room, silent and uneasy. Paula said: *Did it go okay?* I nodded and looked at the floor. Gaia rose from her spot on the stairs and said: *Come on, girls.*

Cassie had been told she was to stay at the hotel. She sat leaning against the fountain wrapped in a blanket when we walked by, her ballet shoes shimmering beside her. On the gravel in front of her was a cup of hibiscus tea. She reached for it and brought it to her mouth. She seemed tired. Alba leaned over and kissed her on the cheek. Cassie smiled softly and said: *Hurry back.* We continued across the courtyard, where earlier in the day we had set up three female figures made of straw that we, not knowing why, had dragged home from a nearby farm the night before. Floating in the trees were what at first glance looked like demon faces, but which turned out to be lacquered buffalo heads carved from oak and suspended by sturdy ropes.

)

We waited a long time for the cable car. The afternoon was in-
digo and warm. Alba's face glowed in the low sun. She had filled
in her eyebrows, they were thicker than usual. Her mouth was
dark purple, like something out of a painting, and looked like an
artificial fruit, more perfect than anything to be found in nature.
The cable car appeared, and we whooshed over the treetops.
Around us the rocks rose to the sky, which seemed endless. In
the valley, work was still ongoing. We heard the sound of hands
and machines. I thought of my mother. Her hands as she worked.
Hands that folded cloth, hands that got pricked by needles,
hands that compelled a complicated machine. From the valley a
light mist rose. A bell could be heard jingling, as always a bell
could be heard in the mountains. In a few hours, all would fall
silent and the festivities would begin.

In Strega, the streets had been covered with a black and fragrant earth. Glazed pots were set out. Parlor palms and fine

carob trees reaching for the sky. Garlands and lanterns hung from the trees. Along the streets, women stood tying large bundles of dried sage to stakes that they had driven into long rows. Children's masks hung around their necks on pink cord. The moment the sun sank behind the mountains, devoured by some soft and ancient darkness that seemed to live back there, the lanterns above us lit up, one by one, giving off a harsh but beautiful light. In the gleam of the lanterns, we looked like something in a department store window, something shiny in plastic packaging that money could buy. We walked through the empty streets letting our eyes absorb everything. Paper flowers and real flowers. Strega dressed for a masquerade. Rock crystal and purple and the jingling of the bell.

We walked toward the mine, the face of which was turned to Strega, the mine shaft like a mouth open onto the underworld. We walked up to a door marked WAREHOUSE and went in. Inside a glass-walled office sat a woman in work clothes sorting envelopes according to what looked like a strict system. She didn't look at us, she counted silently. She was blond and very tall. Perhaps ten years older than us. Perhaps the same age, but marked by the strenuous life inside this terrarium. We stood outside the glass box and waited. She counted, she didn't look up. Finally, Alexa said: *Rex sent us.* She gave a twitch, got up without lifting her gaze, and retrieved a key from a metal cabinet mounted on the wall behind her. She handed us the key, and we handed her the receipt. *Hotel Olympic* in large print against the yellowed paper. She said nothing, but pointed to a door on the other side of the glass box. That's where we went.

The doll lay in a chest, which was perhaps more of a coffin, the lid made of clear plastic. It was an anonymous face that had seen everything. The body was that of a young woman, but the eyes were as dull as the eyes of a corpse. Lorca lifted the lid and ran a hand through her hair. She withdrew her hand and said: *It must be from a person.* We leaned forward, looked down on that stiff face. A foul smell rose from the coffin. Something at once human and synthetic, like the smell of a children's hospital. Alba pressed her fingers to the doll's mouth to see if she was breathing. For a moment, it looked like she was smiling. Paula shut the lid with a bang. We looked over at the glass box, where a phone had started ringing insistently. We looked at each other. Barbara and Alexa lifted up the coffin and carried it through the warehouse. The woman didn't look up as we passed, as if she had forgotten that we existed or wanted to avoid seeing what we were carrying.

We dragged her through Strega. She was heavy, and it was now dark. Bambi had tossed a shawl over the coffin to spare us her face. We stood around the coffin as we waited for the cable car. Her presence was like a strange threat. We convinced each other that she wasn't real, that someone had made her with their hands, that she was artificial and therefore not evil, as if the artificial isn't always more evil than what comes from the earth. I lifted the shawl and looked into her eyes. We heard the sound of engines in the hills, but no men appeared. The cold seized the body and made it bend unnaturally. We climbed aboard the cable car. We held the coffin between us, we said nothing.

)

In the park, lanterns had been lit in the trees. The water in the fountain glittered, illuminated from the side by a stormy fire. From the kitchen window, we heard Rex laughing. We had never heard her laugh before. We carried the coffin into the lobby and set it by the reception, as Costas had asked us to do. We hurried up to the dormitory to change, then rushed down to the ballroom to make it in time for the first service.

There were mirrors everywhere and padded green velvet benches lined the walls. The terrace doors were open, and the fake snow drifted in, because of the wind machine we had placed out there earlier in the day. The room slowly filled with people. All the guests were dressed in black and came bearing gifts, in the form of dried grapes and herbs and other items from the harvest. Rex received them at the door. We served malt bread and meat and fortified wine. We served preserved fruit and cream, chestnuts. We brought in artful pastries with little figures in crystallized sugar. We poured a special drink made from monk's pepper into large pitchers.

Toni, Costas, and Rex walked around in their crushed velvet. The rest of us were dressed as widows, in black cotton dresses, hair gathered at the nape of the neck and hidden by black kerchiefs with the hotel emblem. My mouth tasted of soil. I felt like a heavy mystical moon after the rain. Something moving through space, falling. When I passed Alba holding a platter, she whispered: *I wonder who you'll dance with tonight.* I laughed and walked on, picking up empty glasses and dirty plates from the serving tables and carrying them off to the dumbwaiter. I carried around a tray with small glasses of dark liquor. I averted my eyes when the men addressed me. I smiled and nodded when the women did the same. I saw Bambi flinch when a young soldier grabbed her by the arm. I saw Lorca bare her teeth when a man our fathers' age asked her to sit on his lap. I saw Paula lean forward and whisper something to a man in uniform. I saw Gaia spill hot water over a group of medical students. I saw Alexa spit after a man who stroked her thigh. I heard Cassie hiss something foul when a young man asked her to bend over. I saw Barbara pull the gold cross from her neckline when a priest tried to kiss her hand. I saw Alba stamp on a man's foot hard and pretend it was an accident.

When the service had ended, we were free. They let us eat things with our bare hands. Pickles, bread. We hung out on the benches. We chewed gum, smoked cigarettes, and drank vodka. We watched the guests, judged their choice of attire. Sent long glances to a couple of beautiful young people who looked like they belonged to the theater company. I searched for the murderer, but couldn't see him anywhere. I raised my glass to my lips and leaned my head against the wall. When I shut my eyes, I saw various things making an entrance. Black fabrics falling through rain. Dirty water in a pink bathtub. A scene in which I held a grown man's hands. A scene in which I held my mother's hands. A scene in which I brushed a boy's hair. A scene in which I brushed a rug. I brushed a horse. I brushed a coat. I opened my eyes, grabbed hold of Alba. We sat contemplating the party together. People dancing and laughing. People drinking cloister liqueur straight from the bottle. People feeding each other small, spiced biscuits. We listened to their conversations. Someone said: *Winter will be cold, like winter in Vienna.* Someone claimed to remember the ice rink, melting, and the hands. Rathausplatz, which was silent as a tomb, but gleaming. I saw: children skating in wide circles. The ice steaming, silent and matte and bathed in light.

At midnight, Toni rang a large bell. There was an expectant hush. We stretched to catch a glimpse of Cassie, who was watching us through a gap in the theater curtain. The guests took their seats on the old folding chairs we had lined up in rows in front of the stage. We took a seat on the floor at the edge of the stage, close together. From the open windows came the smell of fire and grass. The moon hung close to the mountains. A quiet murmur came from the audience. I took out my pocket mirror and ran my finger over the small crack in the glass. From my hands came the scent of thunder and violets, the smell of aspirin. Above us the chandelier twisted slowly on its own axis. I ran my hand through my hair and put the mirror back in my pocket.

There was a tinkle, and the overhead lights went out. Alba whispered: *It's time.* The curtains parted with a screech. The stage was lit by a spotlight and decorated like a girl's room from another time. There was pink wallpaper and a jewelry box shaped like a seashell. In the middle hung an oval mirror flanked by kerosene lamps. Cassie made an entrance in a small hat and a dark green dress made of fake silk. One could tell by her face that she was returning from the very first ball of her life. She walked slowly across the stage on her tiptoes with a rose in her hands. She fell backward onto a bed and fell asleep. The rose in her hand dropped to the floor that was covered with a thick rug in a harmonious pattern. It was then that Rex, dressed as a ghost, showed herself in the window, which faced a woody garden. She climbed into the room and approached Cassie, who, still asleep, got up and danced with her. It was strange choreography. Stiff movements in perpetual repetition. Cassie seemed mechanical, as though someone were guiding her movements from a control room somewhere. In the background, something was suddenly illuminated from above. It was the doll from the coffin. She had been concealed behind the dressing table with her face turned away. They had dressed her up as Cassie. Her eyes shone eerily and seemed strangely alive. In the dimmed lighting, Cassie and the doll were identical. The ghost let go of the girl, who fell to the floor like a rag. He turned to the doll with an imploring and enamored gesture. With outstretched arms, he walked to the doll and lifted it up. Simultaneously, Cassie began performing a dance on her back in the middle of the stage floor. She writhed, as if in pain, and let her hair fly around her face like the mane of a horse when it gallops through the night. The tinkling began again, in time with her movements. At first it sounded soft and still, but then it went faster and faster, until it sounded like a single protracted, despairing note. Cassie stretched her arms and legs toward the ceiling and lay like that for a moment, before disappearing through a hatch hidden in the rug. Rex and the doll danced across the stage, over to the spot where Cassie had just disappeared. It was an exact imitation of the dance the ghost had just performed with the girl, but somehow more alive. After a while, he carried the doll to the bed, where previously the girl had been sleeping. He kissed her lips before slipping out the window again. The doll woke up, she got up. She picked up the rose from the floor and kissed it. Curtain.

Applause rang out. It was a harsh sound that bounced off the ceiling and echoed metallically. My fingers prickled from clapping so much. Behind me someone shouted: *Bravo!* I turned around and looked right into the murderer's face.

He pulled me up from the floor, and we walked through the room. He gave me a glass, and I drank. He said: *Do you remember when you came to the spa hotel, when we dove into the water together, your green bathing suit.* I opened my eyes wide. We had never been to a spa hotel together, I don't know who he was talking about, another girl in another bathing suit. I'd never stayed in a hotel in my life. If I went swimming, it was in the lake or in the sea or in the public swimming pool.

We've never been to a spa hotel together, I said, fixing his gaze. He looked at me with something like astonishment. He said nothing, leaned back, and laughed out loud. An orb hung in the air between us, something magnetic and compelling, like a sort of concentration, deep red and golden. My mouth tasted of poppy juice, greasy and nauseating and like something in spring. I asked if he wanted to dance. He took my hand and dragged me onto the floor.

We danced and danced. Everything spun around me. The mirrors and the smoke and the roar of the music. I looked at him. He had a faded tattoo on the inside of his wrist. I brought it to my face and pressed my mouth to the ink. We laughed. We drank and drank. We ate chewy caramels and cherries and bread. I thought: If only I were wearing my confirmation dress.

Each time he looked away, I studied his face. Night had come creeping and settled over his eyes. He was very beautiful in the dark. I felt indifferent and excited. I thought of the nights back home, when my parents were asleep and I was listening to the radio alone in the kitchen. The radio played dance music. There was always a woman's voice singing. Here the music rang hollow, as if it came from the walls. I stood on my tiptoes and whispered: *Come on, I'll show you the park.*

I walked through the lobby with my arms out wide. The floor felt soft and damp beneath my feet. I felt sick. I walked over and leaned against the mirrored wall. I shut my eyes and breathed. Swallowed and swallowed and pressed my forehead to the glass. I opened my eyes and looked right into my own face. Leaves were stuck in my hair. The makeup had run down my cheeks like tears. I looked like a horror character from some old film. I smiled to myself. Inside the mirror, everything seemed to shrink and swell at an uneven pace. The laceleaf on the reception desk doubled in size, only to shrink into miniature in the next moment. I wiped my face with my sleeve. My dress smelled of men's cologne. Sandalwood and amber and black roses.

I braced myself against the wall and started for the dormitory. All along the stairs to the upper floor were fabrics in garish colors. Everywhere, burned-down candles and emptied glasses. Everywhere, the smell of tobacco and spirits and coffee gone cold. In the corridor, the lamps were lit as usual. Cigarette butts and cloth napkins lay on the wall-to-wall carpet. Someone had dropped a glove. Here and there, a fallen garland or some silver lamé. Carnations and evening primrose and decorated masks. It was a beautiful chaos. I felt an urge to take a photograph so as not to forget. I stood there looking at the mess for a while. My fingertips prickled and my eyelids felt heavy. I wanted to vomit but didn't.

I rinsed my face with cold water and brushed my teeth with my index finger. I plucked the leaves from my hair. Put on a nightgown that was hanging to dry over the bathtub. The tap was dripping. I reached out my hand and twisted. I filled the toothbrush glass with water and drank. Hit myself in the face twice.

I walked through the dormitory and took a seat in the window. I breathed in the dawn air, which was light and cool and tasted fresh. The gravel crunched below. I leaned out. Someone was crossing the park, heading for the gates. The dawn was gray like the dawns at home. It smelled of burned plants and of the lake. The sun was still hidden behind the mountains, it hung close to the earth. The moon was up. In the park, people were sleeping. On the table was a cake that had been eaten straight from the platter. Costas went around collecting glasses and plates. I saw a glass ashtray that had fallen from the stone balustrade into the gravel. I saw a tree that suddenly seemed gigantic in the gray light, as if it were being filled up from the inside by the morning, making it swell. The booze still coursed through my blood like an evil grace. I considered vomiting out the window but didn't.

I turned around and looked out over the others. White blankets and black hair and the sound of them breathing. It was hard to see in the dimness, and my eyes were hazy. I lit the storm lantern that stood on the windowsill. Burned my finger on the flame and stuck it in my mouth. I slid down from the window and walked through the dormitory. Held the light up over the beds as I passed them. Everything seemed to be as usual. The deep breathing, the rustling of the sheets.

I held up the lantern over Bambi. Her face bore traces of her makeup, eyelids red and purple, as if bruised. I held up the lantern over Alexa. She slept with an eye mask that made her look like one of the fallen on their way to the kingdom of the dead. I held up the lantern over Gaia. She slept passionately, arms folded over her head. I held up the lantern over Cassie, expecting to see her serious face, the sleep that had settled over it like sheer fabric. I held up the lantern over Lorca, over Barbara, over Paula. I bent over Alba and kissed her on the forehead. She smelled sweet, like plum wine. I lay down in bed. I tried to close my eyes, but the nausea kept overwhelming me, sitting on my chest like a mare. I fell asleep and woke up and fell back asleep. Drunken sleep was a deep river that made me think of death.

I sat up with a jerk, suddenly wide awake. It was as if my body knew something that the brain hadn't registered. I took out my lighter and quickly crossed the room. Held up the little flame above the beds and counted. Gaia, Barbara, Lorca, Paula, Alba, Bambi, Alexa. Gaia, Barbara, Lorca, Paula, Alba, Bambi, Alexa. Gaia, Barbara, Lorca, Paula, Alba, Bambi, Alexa. Cassie was gone. I rushed over to her bed and tore the covers off, my hands searching the sheets, as if she might appear there, doll-size, hidden under the pillows. At first I didn't understand.

The bed was otherwise untouched, as it had stood since early morning, when the sun billowed in through the window like flames. I crawled across the bed and pressed my hands to the wallpaper above the headboard, convinced for a moment that she had been swallowed by the wall. My body let out a strange sound, a sort of gasp that seemed to stifle itself. I walked over and shook Alba. She woke up slowly, as if I had to tear her from a dream. I whispered: *I can't find Cassie.* At first she didn't understand what I was saying. *I can't find Cassie.* I repeated it again and again, until something seemed to flash in her eyes, which gleamed dark and warm in the flame of the lighter. She sat up in bed and shook the sleep off. *What are you saying*, she said sharply. Around us the others woke in a collective movement. They sat up in their beds. *What are you saying*, Alba said, *what are you saying.* Someone switched on the ceiling light. Cassie's bed stood in the middle of the room, perfectly arranged, like a crime scene.

We stood around it and stared. Her nightgown and her hairbrush, her dressing gown flung over the headboard. No one said anything, until Lorca said: *Girls.*

We pulled on thick sweaters over our nightclothes and shoved our feet in our boots. We walked through the Olympic's corridors whispering her name. Bambi said: *We'll find her, she's only met someone, we'll find her.* We walked up the stairs, we walked down the stairs, we whispered her name. We opened closet doors and cellar hatches. We thought we saw her in the mirrors of the ballroom. We thought we saw her behind the curtains in the staff refectory. I heard someone whispering and thought it was her. We paired off and searched the park. We looked in the herb garden. We looked at the edge of the woods. We dragged a net through the green waters of the swimming pool. We dug into the earth, lifted away low-hanging branches, confused various things for her eyes. We took each other's hands and released them, leaned for a moment against the facade and breathed. We walked through the building, we whispered her name. Many hours passed, white and frightening, and the mountains seemed to come closer and closer. We congregated by the fountain, sat down. Someone handed out cigarettes. Someone passed around a lighter. We sat in a thick haze. Around us the dawn light was dry and blue as ice. I reached for Alba, but she turned away.

The information we had was this: Cassie had been at the hotel all day. She had said almost nothing, which was worrying in retrospect. She usually talked a lot, she usually laughed loudly and smoked often, she usually ran her hand through her hair. She had been quiet, she had leaned against a wall and lingered there. She had sat by the fountain. She had combed her hair and gathered it into a perfect bun in the middle of her head. She had worn her dancing dress. She had said: *I'm going to rehearsal.* She had stayed at the Olympic while the rest of us went to Strega. She had walked through the halls wrapped in her blanket. In retrospect, everything becomes evidence that isn't. She had looked right at me and given a short laugh.

Paula said: *I remember walking up to her and asking for a cigarette. I had a glass of amaretto in my hand. She said: I don't have one. I raised my eyebrows. That was all.* Gaia had sat behind the curtains of the terrace doors for much of the evening. She liked the muffled sounds of the park outside. She liked sitting hidden among people. Through a gap in the fabric, she saw Cassie's hand. She said: *It was a pearl necklace or a rosary. It was impossible to tell. The beads were blue and seemed phosphorescent.* She had seen Cassie's hand wrap itself around the string of beads. The skin was taut across her knuckles, and she was sweating. Barbara said: *I suddenly began to feel very sick. Around me the world was a scary movie. I went outside. I sat down. It was cold. I leaned back, lay my head on the grass, and noticed that everything was spinning. In my mind, I saw scenes from another life. Great halls filled with things, my hope chest, china, a small animal I apparently loved very much. I was on the verge of sleep, as if my body wanted to anesthetize me to spare me from the nausea. I remember Cassie's voice in the darkness and there being something in it that sounded like rage, but might have been fear.*

When Barbara fell silent, we just stared at her. Above us, the sky turned from blue to pink, it was morning. We looked at each other through the streaming fountain. Everything sparkled. Nobody said anything. Over at the convent, the nuns' church bell began to ring, it sounded like a funeral. We looked at each other. I said: *I'll get coffee.* The others nodded. I got up and crossed the gravel. Inside the hotel, I caught sight of things I had never seen before. Double mirrors, tapestries, porcelain vases. I paused in front of a window. The harsh light of day flowed across my face. I wanted the landscape to point her out to me, but it was mute. I went down the stairs to the kitchen. Around me everything felt alive. I touched a wall, and it touched back. A repulsive softness to it all. Letter openers with cloth-covered handles. A pistol in a holster made of fur or silk.

In the kitchen, a tap was dripping into an empty ice bucket, which echoed metallically. I boiled coffee and arranged a tray. Nine cups and nine napkins. A jug of milk mixed with cream and a bowl of sugar cubes, individually wrapped in paper with the hotel emblem. Only when I got back to the fountain did I realize that I had set the tray for Cassie too. It looked like a ceremony. I poured the coffee and distributed the cups. I placed two sugar cubes in Cassie's cup as usual. We sat staring ahead. No one said anything. We watched a red light rise from the grass and take the form of a hand. I knew it was the blame and the distribution of blame. I looked at Alba. Her eyes had an eerie shine.

I carried the tray back to the kitchen and washed the cups thoroughly. On my way through the lobby, I stopped in front of the mirrored wall, where there was still the greasy mark from my forehead. Some hours before, I had stood right there, but in another dimension, where nothing yet had the chance to break. I stood awhile taking in my reflection before joining the others, who had congregated in the ballroom with the cleaning equipment.

We picked up fallen garlands, empty bottles, filled ashtrays. We opened the windows wide. We vacuumed and washed the floors with soft soap. We gathered up forgotten objects and placed them in a shoebox. We gathered up the cloths and boiled them. We ironed and mangled. We wiped the doll's face with a rag and pulled a sheet over the coffin. We rinsed the potted plants and placed them in rows. We let our hands repeat the same movements. We listened to the radio, we smoked. We stood in a row by the windows and stared out into the park. It seemed unchanged. A sparse hail fell toward the grass and landed, like pearls. A cold sun lit up the lawn and made it shimmer. The steam was gone, as if swallowed by the earth. A bird sang from its perch in a tree. The fountain shut off, as if someone had pressed a button. It became so oddly quiet. Just then, we were struck by panic. It was like opening one's eyes and finding one's self locked in a cage of polished steel. *CASSIE*, screamed Alexa screamed Bambi screamed Alba screamed Paula screamed Gaia screamed Barbara screamed Lorca screamed I.

Through the building, hard and fast footsteps sounded. Rex appeared in the doorway, wearing men's pajamas. We turned toward her. For a moment, we were a collection of blinking dolls staring blindly. Rex looked at us. She shouted something through the building. We heard footsteps on the stairs, and Toni burst into the room. She stared at us and we stared at her. There was a question in her eyes. We said nothing. The moment seemed eternal. We heard the water rushing through the pipes. We heard the floor creak. We saw an evil spirit walk through the room. Toni smiled a strange smile and ran a hand over her eyes. Her voice was sharp and merciless: *What have you done with Cassie?*

There was a postcard in the grass below the dormitory window. I bent down and picked it up. It depicted the city of Trieste, illuminated from below, as if by a subterranean light. In the canal, the water was aqua blue and turbulent. A high and vibrating summer sky hung over the city. Children and dogs everywhere. Vegetation everywhere. Glasses filled with bright red drinks. Across the picture, a garland and the text *Saluti da Trieste!* in pink. On the back, someone had written in pencil: *Meet me, love, when day is ending.*

In the evening, a ground search was organized. We congregated at the gates facing the forest. Rex's eyes appeared through the darkness, oddly indifferent. Men and young boys had been summoned. They arrived in their woolen sweaters and big boots. They looked like extras in a theatrical performance about the Red Army. Soldiers in enlarged hunting gear. They didn't look at us, I could see it was demonstrative. They nodded silently to each other. I studied their faces and tried to decide whether they were trustworthy people or dishonest people, bedeviled by the place and the poison and the hard life in the hard mountains. The ground felt hard under my shoes. I heard someone say that the night was to bring frost. In a flash, I saw the frost flowers spread like a disease across the windows and Cassie's face.

We walked in a row through the woods. The shadows were long, shifting from blue to purple. The greenery darkened and darkened. Curious shapes became visible in the sky. I ran my hands over each tree I passed. The bark felt dry but alive. I had been placed between Barbara and Paula. I heard them forget to breathe, just like me. I caught Barbara's strong smell of sweat and pepper. The forest vibrated around us, as if it held secrets and hidden signs. The air felt fatty in my mouth, I swallowed. My pulse was high, and there was a buzzing in my ears. Boots knocked against rocks and sank into the moss. We waded through a stream, where the water was cold and reached past our shins. The evening grew darker and darker. In the end, all we could see was what was lit up by Paula's dim flashlight. A thin beam of light that struck rocks and tree trunks and made the forest seem haunted. The fear sank deeper and deeper inside me. We searched and searched, but she was nowhere to be found. My eyes searched for the pattern of her dress. Sometimes it appeared as a replica in nature. Fragile little leaves edged with frost. Dark green polyester. *She's alive, she's alive*, I repeated to myself like an incantation. Everywhere I looked, shapes turned up and disappeared. I flinched each time I thought I saw a face or a hand. We searched and searched. Now and then a man called out through the woods. I thought: *Why did we bring the men, what do they know about death?*

We approached the mountains, which stretched toward the sky like great granite-hewn pillars. We had been walking for an hour when we reached a glade, where a stream babbled on, as if nothing had happened. All around us were rock crystals and darkness. We heard women's voices. We saw shadows that seemed to belong to real bodies. Black coats with white details. A flickering oil lamp lit up a pair of shiny shoes. It was the nuns. Side by side they stood, leaning against the wall of rock. Their faces were serious and collected under the pall. The abbess said: *Rex.* She said: *We're looking for the missing girl.* Her voice was soft, like nothing I'd ever heard before. Something featherlight that flew through the woods and landed. They looked like Saint Quiteria and her nine sisters. I could see the mountain devouring her, the source springing from where her body had vanished.

Rex shouted: *Let's turn back.* Her voice was furious, but also fearful. The abbess turned to the nuns and said something. They set their lanterns down on the ground so that the rock face was illuminated from below. Then, in a single, synchronized movement, they lifted their hands and pointed at Rex. They stood like that for a long time, in silence, before they began to read something in Latin. It sounded like a curse, but it must have been a prayer. The abbess stood in the middle, as self-possessed as a general. I picked out the nun from the forest among the others. I tried to make eye contact, but her gaze was somehow turned away. Behind us, the men started shouting things at each other. Rex just stood there staring, as if paralyzed. No one did anything. The moment just wouldn't end. Finally, Bambi walked over and whispered something to Rex. She flinched and then looked at us, her eyes wide. She shouted: *Let's go!* My legs refused to move. I wanted to stay with the nuns, stand by the rock face and vanish among them, sleep lightly on a bed of stone, only to wake in the dawn, frozen stiff but alive. I wanted to take deep drinks of holy water and eat sacred herbs straight from the ground.

Alba took my hand and pulled me along. The others were already gone, and we had no flashlight. Behind us, the nuns' prayer was still audible, but muffled, as if through fabric. We walked back through the forest. Waded through swamp and moss and ice-cold water. We tripped and fell and stood up again. Followed the voices of the others, until the illuminated windows of the Olympic appeared through the trees. In the park, the fountain was still shut off. The men were leaning against the stone balustrade, smoking. Nothing was real anymore. In the lobby, Costas had set out coffee and spirits. Her eyes were red, and it looked like she'd been crying. She had fetched apples from the cellar, which we cut into wedges and ate from side plates. We drank plum wine from coffee cups. Rex handed out small pills from a box she kept in her breast pocket. We went to bed and slept a benumbed sleep.

When she had been missing for three days, something happened. We woke up, and the dormitory was filled with an impenetrable fog. There was a smell of slaughterhouse. There was a smell of smoke rising from a crackling pyre. In one fell swoop, everything had been eclipsed. The terror of the first two days had also carried with it the will to action of the first two days. An exhilaration that made us make phone calls, brew tea, hand out aspirin and blankets. With the third day came the paralysis of action. It made our hands drop down to our sides and stay there, incapacitated and turned toward the ceiling.

I lay with my head on the pillow, and my body was a stone, a pillar of salt. There was something growing inside me, a silent and cold plant that had taken root below the solar plexus and was now creeping through my body, forcing its stalks in where it could, filling me up from the inside, until I was no longer a person but a container, a glass orb that held something remarkable, a girl being devoured by an internal poisonous plant, an eerie exhibit no one wanted to touch.

Rex came to the dormitory and saw that no one had gotten up. We were as if in a medically induced stupor, as if we had eaten of a sleeping powder distributed in small doses during the night. We were a common thought: *She's never coming back.* There was nothing we could do. Rex's voice, as if underwater, when she called for the others, issued orders about smelling salts and strong drinks, tobacco leaves. Shapes moving through the room. Worried voices. A telephone ringing. Someone pressed a cold cloth to my forehead, someone bathed my lips with gin. Alba reached out her hand and touched mine: *I had such a strange dream.*

The trees outside the window began to rustle softly. I lay looking out over the dormitory. There was a glittering darkness in it all, as if every object had drunk of a starlit night. Rex came up to me, striding across the room like an officer: *Rafa, I want you to inform the other girls that it is time to return to work.*

The men arrived with tools and uniforms. They put a red plastic tape around the entire hotel. I stood and watched it happen. Next to me was a notice nailed to a tree:

GIRL MISSING STOP NINETEEN YEARS OLD
STOP BLACK HAIR STOP BROWN EYES STOP
A HEART-SHAPED BIRTHMARK STOP

It worried me that the notice was handwritten. It worried me that we were surrounded. One could walk into the mountains in patent leather shoes, swim across the lake in her coat, walk through the forest at night. But one could not follow the usual path, get on the cable car, buy a pretzel at the train station. One could not leave this evil place. One could lie down in the woods, let one's hair flow over the moss. One could lie down in bed, let one's hair flow over the pillow. One could lie down there and wait, hear someone coming with a knife or a snare, see his shoes appear under the door.

I wondered who it was that walked the corridors each night. I'd asked the others, but they said it was all in my head. This was the end of the discussion, but he kept returning each night.

We gathered around the tarot cards at the same time that the nuns gathered around the Eucharist. They had wafers and wine. They had incense and eternity. They opened their mouths and received his body. What we had: perfumes, jewelry, magical stones. We drew on each other with pieces of coal we found in the gravel outside the mine. Angular symbols across the chest and cheeks. We drank and ate. Vodka and gummies, sacred food. Inside the evening was a secret that could not be uncovered. Barbara wore a white dress. I touched it, and my hands electrified. Alba nestled in her blanket. I reached for her, and she ran a hand across my forehead. Paula said: *Quiet, it's time.* She dipped her hands in a bowl of moon water. She cast a circle. She called the quarters: east and west. On a cloth she had laid out sage and coal, candles and water, salt. The room was dark. Voices could be heard in the kitchen. It was Rex and Toni drinking their evening coffee. Their moment around the table. In the lobby, Costas was talking on the phone. We held each other's hands. There was the smell of resin. Paula spoke the incantation and a globe took shape before our eyes. Inside the globe:

A rotating billboard showing the Alps, snow-capped.

Facades with vermillion window frames.

A wedding dress hanging to dry over a bathtub.

A postcard from Europe's most famous dance school.

Someone crossing rain-soaked streets at night.

A lamp lighting up a sacristy.

Someone drying their hair with a bright yellow napkin.

Someone asleep in the back seat of a car.

A taxi driving through the woods and lighting up a path.

A girl in uniform.

A luminous triangle above a hotel elevator.

An oak spreading its branches.

Funeral flowers in metal vases.

Something passed through the room. It wasn't Cassie, but something else. Someone screamed. I got up quickly and turned on the light. Alba blinked. I could see she was scared and mournful. It was silent for a while before Bambi said: *I don't understand.* Lorca replied: *Don't understand what?* And Bambi said: *All these images. Red objects and mountains and shadows. I don't understand.* Alexa said: *They were all bad omens.* Bambi looked at her. Alba said: *Women are drawn to all things earthly. Bitter soda and red herbs, a lipstick in a bitter red shade. And death, of course.* Outside the window, it started to rain. Gaia said: *We can't rely on the men, we have to keep looking ourselves, they'll never find her, because they didn't know her.* We nodded. Alba said: *We all know that she's dead, but we need to find her body, so we can wash her and dress her and lay her to rest. So that we can remember her and honor her memory. One must be allowed to bury one's dead.* We nodded.

Outside the window, the rain intensified. It hammered against the window, small children's hands pounding the glass of an aquarium. Muffled steps could be heard on the carpet out in the corridor. Gaia said: *How long has it been raining like this?* Alexa replied: *Ten days, ten weeks.* I got up and walked to the window. Out in the park, puddles spread into lakes, which connected with tributaries. The evening grew redder and redder, as if a red powder had been mixed into the blackness of the sky. Maybe the granite quarry was burning. Perhaps someone had set fire to the convent. Ceremonial textiles, altar decorations burning and burning.

One morning, Barbara found her charm bracelet at the bottom of the fountain. Lorca found a hair clip with a metal star—it was in the flowerbed, it must have been hers. Paula came running with her gold chain in her hands. It had been lying in the earth in the herb garden, spreading a curious light. She said: *Like something glow-in-the-dark.* Alexa turned up in the dormitory doorway. She had found her christening spoon among the sheets of one of the beds. She said: *Room seven on the second floor. You know, with the mountain view.* Bambi found her pocket mirror. She had caught sight of a red mouth in the grass. She bent down, saw the mouth grow bigger and redder against the green. It took her a moment to recognize it as her own. It was a pocket mirror engraved with a *C.* Fingerprints on the glass. Gaia found her knife. A fruit knife with a mother-of-pearl handle—it was hidden among the preserves in the kitchen. Everything glittering that Cassie had owned turned up. One beautiful item after the next. Valuable and shimmering objects that we placed on a cloth on the windowsill. We stood in a row and studied them. It was Alba who said: *But where are all the important things.* We searched and searched for all the bureaucratic things, all the dark blue and white things, all the things that were to be introduced to the record as evidence. The pocket book, the identity papers, the notebook. They were nowhere to be found. I was standing with the dirty linens one day, and out of the laundry basket fell something shiny and rustling. Cassie's gold-mounted pillbox, wrapped in eggshell-white tissue paper.

We collected all these things in a box and carried it down to reception. We wanted to call her parents, but Rex forbade us, said that it was silly to worry them unnecessarily, that Cassie would surely turn up, healthy, safe and sound, and entirely herself.

)

I woke up because it was cold in bed. The snow whirled in through the dormitory window. The sheets draped over me like a shroud, and around the bed, the night air was a perfume. It flowed through the room like a ship with no set course. It smelled of carnations and incense and frost, winter burials in the mountains. I walked through the dormitory and woke Alba, let my hair sweep across her face. She opened her eyes. She hadn't slept, and her eyes were glass orbs in the darkness. She took my hand.

We climbed out the window. Around us, the snow hung like powder in the air. We climbed down the facade, gripping the Virginia creeper with both hands. We landed. The sound of our boots in the grass. Since Cassie disappeared, Rex had taken to sleeping in the lobby, to keep any of us from leaving the hotel during the night. The lights were still on in there. The stairs were bathed in the warm glow of the glass lamp on the reception desk. We leaned against the facade and looked out over the park.

We took hold of each other. We walked through the woods, as we had walked through them each night. We searched for her, as we had done each night, as we intended to do until we found her, so that we could bury her in sacred ground, so that we could honor her memory. We walked quietly. We walked through the night as through a curious dreamscape, in which anything might appear. At the lake, I stepped on something soft. It was a toad. At least, it was the body of a toad. I held it in my hands. It smelled strongly of horsehair. I tossed it in the boxwood. At the lakeshore, we took a path we hadn't before. We had been avoiding it, because the trail seemed impossible to walk. We walked quietly. We let our hands hang at our sides. We felt frost on our fingertips, bark on the backs of our hands. We expected to bump against skin, cloth, or hair, the smell of death or exhaustion. For sixteen days, we had wandered at night. Dark nights, early November, we walked and walked. Alba was tired but wanted to keep going. I felt no fatigue but stared like a blinking doll with dead, unseeing eyes made of plastic.

At the most overgrown part of the trail, Alba's foot bumped into something. She knelt down and reached out her hand. She whispered, as if the forest were an enemy listening to our every word: *It's soft and seems human.* I lit a match. My hands trembled. A warm light lit up the night-forest around us. Alba gasped. Whispered: *It's her dress.* I fumbled with the matches, my fingers were frozen and didn't want to obey. I got the idea that Cassie had changed outfits. I saw her in front of me, alone on the path in the winter night, as she pulled off her dress and let it fall to the ground. She pulled on a nightgown made of thick, durable cotton, better suited for death. I lit another match. On the matchbox was a picture of the Bay of Naples in the sunshine. For a brief moment, I saw it before me: the beach umbrella and the bathing boxes, a child on the shore with a dark red ball.

I thought I could hear seawater roaring in the darkness behind the trees. I knelt down and bent over. The dress smelled of henbane. It lay as if fallen from the sky. We reached out our hands and felt the fabric. It was stiff with frost but sticky, as if it had been dipped in salt water. We sat with the dress where it lay in the snow. We said nothing. A long time passed. I heard Alba's breathing. We saw the dawn arrive. The mist spread from a point behind the mountains. The sun filtered through the treetops. We looked at each other in the white light. Alba's face was empty, as if it had been robbed of something important. How quickly a young face becomes ravaged. I imagined my own face as the face of one who is aged, a fallow field.

We folded the dress and walked toward the hotel. We carried it through the forest like something holy. All around us were misty visions and unease. At the lake, we passed the nuns. They were singing at the water's edge, and their voices rose to the sky. Cassie's face hovered in the air before me. I imagined her getting on a train in some dusky mountain town. I imagined her handbag, plastic-wrapped and placed in a filing system, marked with her initials. It was a beautiful dawn, but around us everything turned ugly. The ugly sky and its ugly light. Ugly trees bearing ugly fruit. I looked at Alba, who had begun to sweat in the cold. At the next bend, the hotel appeared. It rose out of the snow that had been falling all night. A morgue beneath the trees.

We dipped the dress in the pool, let it soak up the green water, let it become heavy like a body that had belonged to a bad person. We brought it to our faces, drew in its smell of earth and stale perfume and aquatic plants. We lifted it out of the pool and went to the herb garden, because it was our temple. It was where we carried our offerings. It was there we held our rituals. We had planted basil and verbena, holy plants. We kept the pests away with mint. We put the dress among our plants. I saw that the mistletoe had grown tall. The red berries had fallen and now lay in the snow, glowing. We lit an altar candle that we kept in the bucket of garden tools. The flame was ice blue and flickered faintly. We placed the candle in the snow next to the dress and read a short prayer. Then we walked through the park, where everything vibrated with the particular silence that comes with snow.

We climbed the stone steps to the lobby, stepped over Rex,

who was stretched out on the marble floor, sunk in a benumbed sleep, all the way up to the dormitory, where the others lay sleeping in the cold. Alba carefully rang a little bell. It was a beautiful sound that rose toward the ceiling. The others awoke, stretched under their covers. As soon as they saw us, they widened their eyes in horror. The dormitory resounded with a terrible silence. I watched as a silent and collective scream stiffened between us.

We put on the black dresses and tied mourning bands around our arms. We fixed each other's hair. We pressed our fingers to Cassie's headboard. We walked silently through the room, as if in a procession. We went downstairs and woke Rex, informed her of what had happened. Her eyes seemed dead, but she made an odd movement with her hand. She went to wake the others. Out in the park, the dawn light was slowly replaced by the winter morning's gray and consuming shine. We walked across the grass, which crunched underfoot. We stood and looked at the dress. No one said anything, but Bambi bent down and pressed her mouth to the fabric. Costas came walking through the park with a silver tray in her hands. She poured hot, bitter tea into large cups and told us to drink. I dipped my tongue in the liquid until it began to taste of blood. Barbara was whispering with her rosary in her hand. I looked at Alba, but she turned away. Toni arrived with a bouquet of black dried flowers, black petunia.

We walked back through the lobby, where Rex now sat at the ledger making notes. We walked up to the counter and stared at her until she looked up. Lorca said: *Give us her parents' phone number.* Something moved across the floor, we saw it happen— the steaming walls, the poison powder wafting through the air. Rex said: *Allow us to make the call, we've dealt with this kind of situation before.* We stared at her in horror, until she bowed her head and wrote down the number on the back of a business card.

The phone was made of Bakelite and gleamed against the red wallpaper. Lorca held the receiver a bit away from her ear, so that everyone could hear. *She left, and we haven't been able to find her,* she said. *We haven't been able to find her, but we have found her dress,* she said. *On a path, yes, in the woods, by a grove.* On the phone, a silence unlike anything else. The parents' breathing spread through the phone booth like an evil pulse. The body's formalized prayer, a heavy, steady rhythm, a warning bell. Finally, a voice was heard saying: *We're coming.* A click and then the white noise, in which we immediately began to look for hidden signs, thought we heard someone whispering down the telephone line, a spirit imitating Cassie's voice.

We stood there listening for a long time. We reeled off various prayers we remembered from our childhoods. We walked through the corridors in our black dresses. We looked like a funeral cortege. We looked like a political cell en route to an execution by firing squad. Bridesmaids en route to the altar. We walked in circles around each other, leaned against each other. We drank hot water with lemon. No guests arrived.

They came by taxi. It was a clear, frosty night, and the moon hung over us like an all-seeing eye. We observed them under the cover of darkness. We stood in a row in our uniforms. From the taxi came the sound of a radio playing dance music. In the mountains, there was the clink of icicles and a deep tone, something quaking, as if they were still blasting in the mines, a strange night job, stone after stone crashing through the dark.

Rex received them at the door, dressed in a white shirt and hunting trousers. She had put on the mourning band, which usually lay discarded in the mailbox at reception. She took the father's hand and kissed the mother lightly on the cheek. Whispered something inaudibly and looked her in the eye. She carried their lone bag up the stairs, like a bellboy. We followed them, inside our uniforms, with our anonymous faces and identical plaits. We had spent the day cleaning, had donned black fabric and washed the floors.

They were assigned the suite facing the park. Around Cassie's mother was the smell of shock and moth repellent. I reached out a hand to touch her, but she recoiled, as if I were dangerous. I turned away, it was an automatic movement, my gaze fastened on the wallpaper. Horses and peacocks placed in a treacherous landscape, in which a thick sap ran down the trees and into the grass. My heart pounded in my chest, and my hands trembled. It had never occurred to me that they might be afraid of us.

In the dining room, someone had turned on the electric light hanging from the ceiling. It gave a sullied shine to all the beauty. The silver candlesticks were lined up on the mantelpiece. A black orchid doubled in the mirror behind it. The parents sat next to each other at the table. Costas served clear broth in deep bowls. We studied them from behind a drapery. The mother slowly brought the spoon to her mouth. It seemed oversize in her small hand. The shadow across her forehead made me think of Cassie. The father stared straight ahead. It looked like he didn't know what to do with his face. Tried one grimace after the next before he, as if on command, let his face fall. We could tell that he already knew. We could tell that she nurtured a strong and impossible hope. Then, all night, she walked the corridors. We heard her as she passed our door. A monotone voice that rose and fell in a steady rhythm. She repeated the same words: *It's just her dress. She changed outfits. It's just her dress.*

They would bury her, some years later, in her hometown. Or: They would lower an empty coffin into the earth. Inside the coffin, various objects: the dress, the charm, a lock of hair from when she was a baby. An empty coffin in a family grave or mausoleum. One may imagine a place with low benches and much greenery. Large bouquets of hydrangeas. Old stones. One may imagine a beautiful resting place among plants. I visited the grave once. It was all very barren and very communal. It was a simple grave by a gravel path. There were *arborvitae* in long rows, wilting flowers in cellophane. A porcelain dove in a wreath of porcelain flowers. Above the tombstone, someone had fixed a picture of Cassie. I stared at her and wanted to vomit straight out. Ghost water in the dry earth. It was a child's face. I looked at her round cheeks. Felt an urge to bite them or pinch them warm.

The parents disappeared as suddenly as they had arrived. In the early morning they were picked up by a taxi, identical to the previous one. We stood in the terrace door and watched it happen. Toni had gathered Cassie's things in a box. In an unguarded moment, we had stolen her pocket mirror for ourselves. We knew it was wrong, but we did it anyway. It sat on the edge of the bathtub, glowing like an object washed with holy water, something sacred that was dripping. There were chalk marks on the curved glass. We thought we could see her eyes in there, like two black planets encircled by a beautiful light. Costas said: *We should have sent the things by post. Spared them the long journey.* Rex said: *They wanted to see her bed and the place where she worked. They thanked us for the kindness.* When they had left, her bed stood glowing in the room, like a living grave with a human scent. I touched it each time I walked by. I suspect the others did the same.

One month of mourning passed. The men kept looking for her in the forest. I stood at the gates and saw their hands sweep over boulders and moss. I saw their hands reach for the sky in silent desperation. We knew their work was in vain. Something told us she was actually gone. Maybe she was in the lake. Maybe she was in the earth. Maybe she had hitched a ride with a truck driver to meet someone in an out-of-the-way square, somewhere by a stone wall lined with green plants. We knew she was gone, but it was our secret. We let the men carry on with the hunt. Let their hands honor her in this way.

For us, each day was a ceremony. We made an altar with shiny objects. We lowered a sheet over her bed and sprinkled it with scented water. We pronounced her name in front of the darkened mirror at night. We each put a rosary pea in our uniform pocket.

Each day was a false labor. We sorted things by color and size.

We ran a damp cloth over the clean shelves. We let our hands work without us. The hands remembered how the beds were to be made for the night. The hands remembered how the curtains were to be pulled aside in the morning. The knowledge of the hands is different in every way to that of the head. The hands remember soaps, fabrics, and skin. The hands remember how to make wreath plaits, long after the school years have ended, long after one has cut off one's hair and placed it in a small cotton bag. Long after the hands have stopped lifting up from the lap to reach for the child and the child's hair and instead stay in the lap, dry and slender and turned to the sky. The hands remember what it's like to iron rayon shirts with an electric iron. The hands remember gas flames, cigarette embers. The hands remember the autumn sun beating against them with its particular heat. The hands remember the vise grip of frost. The hands remember Cassie. Her thick hair greasy to the touch.

I stood at the gates and looked out over the landscape. The men were packing up for the day. Axes and flashlights in large canvas bags. Dusk fell, I watched it happen. A pink glow streaming from the sky and mingling with the frost crystals. I heard the abbess shout in the woods: *The evening will be warm, you can all take off your gloves.* I looked down at my hands. Stiff with cold and somehow artificial. Something red fluttered before my eyes. I squinted, it was over by the convent. A dress was hanging to dry next to the well. It fluttered in the wind and revealed its lining, dove blue and decorated with silver thread, secret messages embroidered.

I thought about going home but didn't know how that was supposed to happen. I had tried to write a letter to my mother more than once, but had to give up. I wrote: *Mum.* The ink flowed out and made my handwriting illegible. Perhaps I could no longer speak the language of daughters. I called home and heard the signals go through. I was leaning against the wall in the phone booth. The signals went through, I waited. There was a click, followed by an electric crackle, then her voice arrived. I shut my eyes. Behind the voice was the whole apartment, the kitchen fan and the radio, and behind this was the city with its smell of water, bread, citrus. She said: *Hello.* She said: *Rafa.* I couldn't bring myself to respond. I stood there holding the handset, I was sweating. As if out of nowhere, I heard a voice say: *Nannies for those who don't have parents.*

I opened the gates and started walking through the forest. The snow was deep, it reached my knees. The cold spread from my feet upward, I let it happen. Around me, the greenery was dormant. The tree branches were covered with a thick frost that made them glitter. I walked and walked, until my lips stiffened. I saw that one skated on the frozen lake. It was beautiful in the twilight. I saw that one brought along bread and coffee and fruit preserves. Strong liqueur made from yellow plums. A medicinal scent rose from the snow, as if the white color could give off this scent of powder, of arsenic. I continued through the forest. The lake was candlelit by large lanterns. Someone shouted in the mountains. Someone laughed. In the glow of the lanterns my hands were blotchy and appeared burned, as if I had held them in fire to punish them.

Each night, I thought about my murderer. I imagined a row of beautiful women. Behind them, a row of ugly women. Behind them the stupid women, the intelligent women, the women with fat cheeks. I saw disgusting women, old women, women with empty hands and no rings. I was sure there was a murderer waiting for us all. I drew him in a brown suit and patterned shirt. I conjured him. I had always thought that I would make a beautiful corpse. I would take care not to be ugly when it happened, take care not to become an ugly murder victim, lying there with my mouth open in a dress I had inherited, as much a failure in death as in life. I harbored an internal mechanism that bathed everything in a glittering light, the mechanism that binds death with beauty and beauty with death. It's an unworthy life from the start, this life where the brain is replaced by a corrupted system. Let's say one stares a grown man in the eye in the worst way. Let's say one leaves the mouth open, showing the tongue.

Let's say one has always been a bad woman who deserves ill. I've always liked fur. I've always liked fetuses in formalin.

The murderer pops up throughout life with different faces. In childhood, he lived in the face of the tobacconist, as a threat. This was before I had begun to name this face, before I had understood that he was my murderer. The tobacconist looked at all children with the same rage, but it was only when he regarded me that the rage also contained the disgust that lives in the flesh of every murderer. He looked at me, and he wanted to annihilate me. I stared at the selection of sweets. A blue lollipop, my favorite, stuck to my fingers. I wanted him to knock it out of my hand, so that his brutality would become concrete, so that I could talk about it, introduce it to the record. That never happened. He slunk along the walls, he stared. I rolled a red ball across the floor. It rolled until it bumped into a shoe belonging to a grown person, my father or the schoolmaster, his shoes were shiny, he bent over, tore the lollipop from my tight grip, and paid for it with a coin.

When I turned thirteen, the murderer moved into a new face. One evening during a holiday by the sea, he appeared in the eyes of my father's best friend. What was murderous in him looked different. Within his hatred too, the disgust was planted as a condition, but this disgust also contained a sick desire. I understood that the murderer's inner life operated like one of those dolls that houses several smaller dolls. But which is the innermost doll? This I don't yet know. Perhaps the innermost doll is simply a red and hateful stone with a murderer's face. Something pointless and frightening in every way. On my deathbed, when the murderer has finally come to me with his hands, with his white powder and his knives, I intend to write the answer to this question on my hand, next to his name. Bury me with my hands turned to the sky.

I knew the murderer was never far. I had seen him step out of the walls. I had seen him among the bedsheets. I had seen him in the bathroom tiles, behind the mirror glass. I'd worn him in my bun, wrapped up there like a secret charm containing someone's portrait. A hand that emerged from the hair and took firm grip of the neck. In every woman's life, there's someone waiting at the gate. We are all candidates, but only some of us are chosen. I knew there were holes in the earth waiting for us. Nine holes in the earth, dug to our measurements. We were to lie there, beautiful in our little ladies' coffins, beautiful in our confirmation dresses, which were already too small, tight across the chest and shoulders and no longer clean.

One might have an urge to say: *We would rather be martyrs together than live another second in this order.* One does not. One bides one's time. One waits for one's murderer, one sees him everywhere. One imagines the night it will come to pass. One knows all about that night. One knows the lines. One knows how he follows after, hypnotizes, addresses one in another's voice.

It could be a girl's voice, a boy's voice, a nun's. One is aware of the method he uses to lure one away from the group. One looks down, one discovers footprints in the snow. One sees that they lead into the building, but not out.

I had many fantasies about girls meeting their murderers. An empty airport in southern Germany. A girl appeared in the arrivals hall. She walked quickly, her shoes clacking on the floor. When the automatic doors opened onto the storm, she lost her shawl and a taxi braked. It was the man who was driving. She got in.

I squeezed my eyes shut, and the murderer appeared in my mind. It turned out his face was the face of all men. In his features was every single one. In them the whole lineage was collected in a single person, a chosen dangerous representative, the double agent of men. He was a man who leaned back and looked at one unwaveringly. A man who distributed the sum violence of the lineage with calm, methodical hands. Organized himself against all women. I wanted to lie in his lap and rest. I wanted to ask: *What's the difference between a convent's abbess and a brothel's madam? What did Venus do with the unicorn?* Things one asks oneself though one shouldn't.

I saw before me: A cold institution. Anonymous doors in a long corridor with wall-to-wall carpet and textured wallpaper. One opens a door and there he sits, doling out sentences and punishments, a card index of all the world's failed women, my name in capital letters on the white paper, the institution's stamp glowing blue. A hand that writes: *Introduce to the record that this is a horrid species deserving of ill.* In the umbrella stand in the corner a leather whip. No, it's too much.

)

I woke up at dawn unable to breathe, heart stiff with a single thought: that Cassie could be forgotten, that there would come a day when all this would seem like a peculiar game, that this was how we would tell it to our children, there was a hotel and a peculiar game, come let me tell you.

I decided that I would introduce everything as evidence. I gathered whatever I could find that reminded me of Cassie. A plastic comb, an apricot-pink blush, her brand of cigarette. I made drawings of her bed, how it was situated in the room. I scooped up water from the fountain and poured it into a small bottle. I tore off a piece of her sheet that I thought smelled like her. Then I gathered it all up in my underwear drawer, in anticipation of a tribunal somewhere, where all would be brought to light. I saw the whole thing before me. The judge holding up locks of hair and dress hems in front of a black-clad jury made up of grown men. I was called as a witness, but had been rendered mute because someone had cut out my tongue. In my hands: the evidence. She had existed.

When the sun was at its zenith, I asked the others to line up in front of the fountain so we could take a photograph. I set the focus and ran across the gravel, to make it into the shot before the self-timer clicked. After the picture was taken, we sat down in the gravel and smoked, as we used to do in the beginning, before everything became impossible. We talked quietly and softly. Dreamed up a shared life in which we lived in a beautiful apartment with many rooms, in which we worked and lived and laughed often, in which we drank cold wine, ate fruit, marzipan, reached slowly for slim cigarettes, coffee cups, each other's hands. Someone mentioned Cassie's name, and Lorca said: *I have no words for these feelings.* Alexa waved her hand in the air in front of her, as if to bat away a ghost. We passed the matches around, we smoked, we said nothing.

That night, when everyone was asleep, I developed the photograph in the bathtub. We stood in a row along the fountain in our uniforms. Some smoked, others smiled with all their teeth. Our faces were blurred, like in very old photographs that have faded with time. I had an urge to color it in with red pencil but didn't.

The hotel was no longer a hotel, but a machine of destruction. Disciplinary measures of greater or lesser brutality were put into effect everywhere. The windows shrank in pace with the beds, which grew harder and harder and in the end most resembled sarcophagi. Each day was a horror show in which various phantoms seemed to enter and exit, like mechanical dolls. The hands gathered the hair in an ever-tighter bun. The hands reached for the cigarettes. We automatically arranged ourselves in ritual formations. We watched our bodies do things against our will.

I looked around. Anonymous hotel maids who disciplined themselves. Small even cuts and scalding water. It was unendurable, but we endured.

We saw something wafting through the halls, red air. We filled our lungs with this bitter red, which was irresistible because it was also sweet. If one felt bad, there was a medicine cabinet to rummage in. There were different kinds of vaccines, there were gold salts, there were bottles of cough medicine and quinine. Curious old decoctions with the nuns' emblem printed on the labels of the glass bottles. The threat of a hygienic-dietic cure in a sealed institution. It happened that I drank greedily from a green bottle. I stood next to a curtain, and I became the curtain. I folded sheets, and my hands evaporated. I sat in the bath and let the water cool. I said to my reflection: *You are normal, you have never been anything but normal, your dress and the pleats of your dress.*

I held my hands up to my face and caught their smell of ether and naphtha. As if my body were saponifying. I closed my eyes. In my mind I saw: Bright blue lakes. A funeral gondola. Someone whispering: *Iris.* Someone whispering: *It's a secret.* Three women handing out carnations and leaflets, old buildings and canals, a bottle of perfume smashing against a wall, the smell of ivy spreading through the room. A porcelain figurine lying at the shoreline. A spa hotel, where a patterned fabric wafted through the elevator shaft. Three women in funeral garb and the judge of a children's tribunal. A silver spoon lying against the edge of a plate, shining. I opened my eyes. I had an impulse and tattooed Cassie's initial on my thigh. A sterilized safety pin and dark blue ink. The pain was dizzying.

I lifted the wet cloth from one tub to the other. It was midnight, I was a midnight laundress. I rubbed and rubbed the gall soap into Cassie's dress. It was a stain that refused to let go. It looked like someone had wiped their greasy fingers on the fabric after eating something with their hands, from a paper box of fried meat or deep-fried pastries, something one buys from a street vendor on a red-letter day. When I brought the dress to my face, it smelled of soil and fur, as if it came from a place beyond time. I had already rinsed the dress many times. I longed to bring its hem to my face and for it to smell of scented detergent, of factory, but it continued to stubbornly give off more and more of that smell of soil and corpse and damp fur with each dip in the tub.

It had all begun at dusk. I had been lying in bed and staring at the ceiling, where the spread of red mold was still alarming. Around me the others lay sleeping. Inside my mouth echoed a question. It sounded like it was hitting the walls of an empty, tiled room: *Who washes for the dead, who irons?* When I closed my eyes, I saw a scene in which a young girl was lifting black cloths out of a large laundry basket. It was in a shady enclosed court-yard with greenery and rocks. I observed her washing the night-gowns of the dead by hand. The embroidered coverlet from a dead woman's bed. The question echoed and echoed, until I got up and walked through the dormitory. I walked down the stairs in the soft glow of the corridor's lamps. I walked through the park in the compact darkness. I fetched the dress from its place in the herb garden, carried it across the grass like a bride. I laid it out on the wash table in the laundry room, where the smell of boiling water and linen still sat in the walls. Outside the window lay an impossible night, and from the mine gleamed something yellow and frightening.

I used every method I could think of. Repeated to myself all that Toni had taught me: *Silk is rinsed in a tub with vinegar. Cotton and down are soaked in mild detergent. Buttons are washed in lukewarm water.* I fetched bottle after bottle of cream-colored soft soap. I fetched apple cider vinegar, caustic soda, eau de cologne. I drew my hands through the water. I leaned over the tub. Stared into the water for a while, before bending over and dipping my head in. Under the water, the sounds were muffled and eerie. Something was striking the inside of the tub, and I looked over. The buttons of the dress were tapping against the enamel. I widened my eyes, watched the fabric sweeping through the water.

I stood like that, head underwater, until my lungs began to ache and my body rose as if on its own. I panted and panted, leaning against the tub and gasping for air, letting the water run from my hair down to the floor. Out there was the morning. It had come from the mountains and settled over the park. I looked over.

I removed the dress from the tub and wrung it out. Rolled it in a towel, which became heavy with moisture. Held it up in front of me in the thin light. For a moment, I saw Cassie as she was. Beneath my heart, something hard melted, a lava rock. I went to the park and hung up the dress there to dry on a hanger. The morning was otherworldly. For a few minutes, everything was bathed in a fiery red glow. I saw it happen. Frost flowers, mist, fire. And so, the rich milk of the winter morning flowing and flowing from the high heavens. I looked at my hands, which were ruined from spending hours in hot water. I took a tube of salve out of my pocket and coated them. The smell of camphor and the morning and the dripping of the dress.

I walked through the park with my hands facing out. I walked through the lobby, where the wall of mirrors glittered and glittered, just like everything else that morning. I caught sight of my reflection and gave a short laugh. I looked like some sea monster from a Greek tragedy. My hair lank as seaweed around my face, my eyes radiating. I smiled to myself. Pressed my hand to the mirror and continued up to the dormitory.

There was a game in which one of us hid with a tiny bell. The other was to follow the sound, blindfolded. It was a horrid game. The brittle sound of the little bell and the blind groping hands.

I walked through the corridor blindfolded. I heard the bell, one moment like a distant tinkling in the mountains, the next very close by. Alba moved around me without a sound, like a panther. Could easily make her way down the corridor and back before I had a chance to take more than a few steps. She let her hair sweep past my face. It felt like a cold breeze and a familiar scent that became particularly intense, because the blindfold sharpened my senses.

I kept moving through the corridor and felt the ice gathering in my chest, just below the dip of my throat. The sound of the bell moved back and forth, sometimes it seemed to come from the floor. I heard it behind me, as if it were hanging level with the nape of my neck. Then suddenly, the sound was gone. A resounding silence that bounced off the walls. I said her name. She didn't answer. I said it again. I lingered there, as if frozen in place, fingers cramping, until I heard a dull thud right in front of me. I tore off my blindfold. The light was sharp, and I blinked. In front of me on the floor lay Alba's dress. Not the one she had been wearing, but a different one.

There was a game where we told each other things. We moved into room number seven and locked the door. It was night, and the moon hung over us like a mother. Alba put a little bell over the door, which would ring if anyone tried to get in, like in a shop that sells milk or charcuterie or anything else. The steam from a refrigerated display case. I crushed a drinking glass and placed the shards on the windowsills. We lay next to each other in bed and stared up at the ceiling. Alba told me things, as if she were recounting shared memories from a fabricated childhood. In another cosmos, where we had to sleep next to each other in a narrow, fragrant bed.

She said:

When we were infants, our aunts held us in their arms and said: Bébé. We lay on blankets on lawns. We lay on the beach under para-

sols. Before we were born, the aunts had collected some things in an enamel box with a poppy painted on the lid. There was a feather and a dried rose hip, there was a bottle of nail polish, a pair of golden miniature scissors, there was a piece of light green velvet and a black lock of hair tied with a pink ribbon.

When we were little girls, three or four years old, our aunts came to visit with parcels in their bags and arms. Tissue paper rustling in their hands. They arrived with striped dresses, yellow white pink. They arrived with soft shoes to be worn indoors. They arrived with combs of horn and metal. A brush of bright red plastic.

When we were schoolgirls, the aunts arrived with pencil boxes and rubbers. Small jars of invisible ink. One was somebody when writing with that ink. One wrote, hands and arms full of secret messages.

When we turned thirteen, the aunts arrived with underwear and hairpins. A big box of pink curlers. They read aloud from novels, moral tales of governesses and horses. We were on the hunt for gaps in the story, a child who is in fact a ghost, a window beating through the night, a tree that gives off blood and liquid.

When we turned sixteen, the aunts arrived with sixteen candles and sixteen black silk ribbons. Yellow candle wax dripping on soft hands.

It was a ritual in which our wrists were bound together and we were left to sit on the floor. Backs together, legs straight out. We had taken off our party shoes and lined them up along the wall. There was a cake on a table in the middle of the room. Purple cream, candied lavender flowers, dark blue marmalade between sponge bases.

When we turned twenty-five, they arrived with baby clothes for our unborn children. They whispered: Have the infants wear amulets. Have them lie in cool rooms.

When we died, they chased us across the Red Sea. Sulfur was spread over the place where we had lived.

Alba gave a laugh. A dry little laugh that rose to the ceiling. I smiled and shut my eyes, said: *What happened next?*

On the back of my eyelids, I saw curious scenes from someone else's memory. Smoke rising from a funeral pyre. Fading spring flowers. A box with a butterfly collection, in which the butterflies were made of brittle paper. A cup with a very bitter liquid. A green onyx statuette. The river lay before me, flashing black. Hard rain over a square I had never visited.

I opened my eyes and thought for a moment that Cassie's face was floating in through the window like a luminous orb. I saw her dress cross the carpet. I blinked and turned to Alba:

What happened next?

)

There was a game where we put our hands on each other's collarbones. We'd press our thumbs down and sit like that, until
the blood began to pound in the jugular notch and we blacked
out. I looked into Alba's eyes. They were like crystal balls in
which all could be revealed, if that's what one wanted. We sat
there, silent and stiff and forgotten by the world. It was a wicked
joy. I signaled to Alba, and she let go. She sat looking at me for
a while, ran her finger over the bruises. Placed her hand on my
cheek and sat like that. Said: *Little Rafa*. We heard the water
running through the pipes. We heard the vacuum cleaner and
the mangle. A cold wind came through the window. We leaned
out and looked at the morning dust and glitter. The park lay
empty. I reached out my arm and stuck my fingers in the ivy.
Our hands had left marks on the facade.

Alba said:

I heard that something terrible happened at the Olympic before.

I heard that a man came to the hotel. He had with him cleaning products for sale. He was beautiful or ugly. No one had seen a man in a long time, so no one could know. He wore a silver chain around his wrist. He had coins and bills in his pockets. When they stroked his cheek, his mouth made a strange sound. When they leafed through the book he was carrying, a bundle of letters fell out, the envelopes covered with childish writing. They took off his clothes and rinsed him with hot water, with cold water. They ran ice cubes over his face. They gave him water to drink. They gave him meat and coffee. They made a bed for him in the kitchen. They rinsed his pockets and found a photograph. It was of a young woman shading her face with her hand, leaning against the railing of a tourist boat. He was a man or he was a boy. It is said that they murdered him in a new way each night. How strange that he never showed fear, they whispered to each other: Why isn't he saying anything? Is he already dead? They brought down old sheets from the attic and wrapped him up. They administered poison and waited. Night fell and they lit lamps. He looked tired but seemed to have an incredible life force, singing songs and running his hands through his hair. After a few hours, they held him out in the light. There were stains everywhere. His eyes had changed color and brightened. Someone else had moved into his face. They made small cuts wherever they could. They gave him nothing to drink. They bathed him in hot water. They made him eat nails and wool. They brought in dogs and allowed them to bite at his hands.

The next morning, a young man came walking through the park with his suitcase. He was the first actual guest during our time at the hotel. They said he was called Bastiano. They said he came from one of the cities by the sea, but I didn't recognize him. We suspected that Toni had recruited him from the theater, that they had paid him.

To welcome him, we were to organize ballroom dancing in the ballroom. Toni looked at us and said: *You are lighthearted young women with beautiful laughs.* We just stared at her. She knew very well that we were no longer girls, but something else entirely. We danced with him in shifts. It was reluctant and joyless. The same gramophone record played over and over again. Now and then Costas applauded from her spot at the bar. Bastiano's hands were heavy and sweaty on our hips. While one of us danced, the others sat on the velvet benches along the walls. I wanted to take Alba's hand but couldn't. On the floor there were bread crumbs and dust and cigarette butts. We danced and danced. Alba whispered: *Should we pour water on him. Should we bring in the dogs.*

I sat up that night writing things down in blue ink on pink paper. My night brain spilled out across the pages. From my hands rose the smell of Bastiano's aftershave. A chemical smell that couldn't be washed off. I wrote: *A hotel in the mountains. One passes by. One feels like drinking a glass of something yellow and refreshing, something strong. One stands by the lake. One wants to photograph the view, but doesn't. One hears the surface of the water breaking and looks over. A dead schoolgirl emerges from the depths. Her hair flows out around her head in a beautiful way. And after her others follow. One by one they surface, all the world's missing girls, hundreds, thousands. Some in nuns' wimples, others in uniform. They stretch their hands to the sky. One wants to shout: Where have you been? One wants to shout: We've been looking for you.* I read what I had written aloud to myself, then burned the pages over the bathroom sink.

Bastiano left the next day. He stayed only one night. It was to his credit that he had moved on. I made his bed. I picked up candy wrappers from the floor. I turned off the radio. He had been listening to Radio Moscow. He had left a paper on the bedside table. It was a pencil drawing of the view of the park from the hotel room's only window. It was a section of the park that shone with sharper contrasts than the rest. It was the herb garden. He must have seen it and understood that it was the only thing that was still alive at the Olympic. I folded up the drawing and tucked it inside my uniform.

I stood at the fountain sorting stones by size. Perfect forms that came from nature. I searched everywhere for the murderer's face, convinced he was in the stones or the walls, in the bathwater or the palm of a hand, in the shadows behind the nuns' altarpiece.

Once, I thought he appeared in the ceiling painting in the lobby. He came out of the paint, out of the burned foliage, like something developed in a darkroom. I recognized him by the eyes, which were green and had a fierce power of attraction. I wanted to walk into the painting and disappear. Lie down flat on the yellow grass. Many years later, on a beautiful day in May, the sun hanging heavy over the hotel, they would discover me. A young woman from the seasonal staff would notice a black mark among all the yellow. She would bend over and press her hands to her chest. She would catch sight of me, stiff as a corpse, hands turned to the sky as if in eternal capitulation. My eyes would be open in death, where there is no god, but only a numbed sleep. I would lie there with my hair beautifully arranged around my face. This would be my funeral.

I looked up from the stones and caught sight of Bambi a short distance away in the park. The morning had been foggy, but now it was clearing up. She came walking as if out of the last fog. She looked like a bridesmaid, held in her arms a large cellophane-wrapped bunch of violets. She paused in front of me. She seemed to be inspecting my face, measuring and weighing me, as if to sell me in the market hall of some godforsaken industrial town on the plains. I laughed, briefly and involuntarily. Said: Where did you get that from? She looked at me with great seriousness, before handing me the flowers, and I accepted them with out-stretched arms.

A<small>lba</small> said: *Imagine being a juvenile delinquent.* And I responded: *We're too old to become juvenile delinquents, look at our hands.* And she said: *Juvenile delinquents with old hands. We'd clean out big villas of their money, jewelry, valuable books.*

I pictured our hands digging into jewelry boxes and pulling books off the shelves, letting them fall to the floor like empty children's coffins. And outside the villa, a radiant morning. Something golden streaming in through the burn holes in the velvet curtains. And our hands found a safe and opened it, ran across gold nuggets and bundles of disintegrating love letters tied up with string. Someone's secret, someone's treasure. The heart in my chest, like something raging and alive, brought to life by this work, which was the work of the thief. And we stood in the darkened vestibule and stared into a gilded mirror that stretched toward the ceiling, and inside the mirror, like two hanging moons, our criminal faces shone as if lit up from within.

Maybe, Alba said, *we can find a way out of this crime scene by making one of our own.*

)

I walked through the corridor with the cleaning trolley. An ominous silence hung over the hotel, which made me think that something was going on outside our field of vision. As if confidential meetings were being held in the conference rooms or some secret society was conspiring in the honeymoon suite on the second floor.

Alba was sitting nearby, her back against the cellar door. She said: *Come here, Rafa, sit.* I pushed the trolley to the wall, pulled out a cigarette from the packet I kept among the bottles of polish, and sat down with her. I said: *What are we doing tonight?* She said: *We're going to Strega.* I nodded, took a drag on the cigarette, and handed it to her. We got up and walked to the dormitory, stubbed out the cigarette on the wall so that it made a mark. Left the trolley to sparkle in the afternoon light.

In the dormitory, the others lay on the beds reading and smoking and painting their nails. Paula sat on the floor, bent over cards from the major arcana. I took out an envelope of incense paper, which I kept at the bottom of my suitcase. I lit one sheet over the metal plate that held my jewelry. The paper spread a forest scent around it. Resin and saltpeter and the smell of fire. I sat for a while, breathing in the green and looking at the others. Hollow-eyed girls with things in their hands. Alba said: *Rafa and I are going to Strega.* No one said anything. In the middle of the room, Cassie's bed was shining white. I said: *Who's coming?* Alexa looked up and shook her head. Alba snapped her fingers, as if to wake them. Nothing happened.

We put on civilian clothes and tied black ribbons around our necks. We smoked the waterline of the eye with a piece of coal. We brushed our hair to a shine. We put on clean panties and thin nylon stockings. We put on rings and bracelets. We painted our eyebrows black and our lips oxblood red. When we passed Rex, who was stamping letters in the lobby, she turned away, as if to avoid the sight. We walked past her and through the gate. At the gates, we climbed over the barricade. We walked along the edge of the woods but kept our eyes fixed on a point ahead. We shared a cigarette and smoked in silence. The cable car was still not running. No one was working in the valley, and it was silent at the mine. We spent a while taking in the view. It was magnificent. I stubbed out the cigarette on the hotel sign, took out two pieces of chewing gum, and handed one to Alba. We stood by the mountain road and waited, sticking out our thumbs each time someone drove by. Everyone honked at us but kept driving. Finally, someone stopped. I leaned over and looked through the window, where a tree-shaped air freshener was dangling from the rearview mirror. Behind the wheel was a woman about my mother's age. I breathed out and signaled to Alba. We hopped in, and the woman drove us very quickly and very recklessly down the mountain in complete silence.

We arrived just as the streetlights were switching on along the high street. Lamps were hanging all around. We didn't see a single person. We passed the train station and the flower shop. Everything in there was dead, except what was plastic. An artificial monstera in a red-glazed pot. We stopped in front of the souvenir shop's window. Porcelain figurines, gemstones, and cutlery. We stood so close to it our breath fogged the window. In the left corner, behind a children's coffee set, I caught sight of an open amulet. Inside the amulet was a miniature oil painting. The subject was Ophelia among water lilies, hands turned to the sky, hair like a fan in the green water. I got it into my head that her face was Cassie's face. The same fluvial darkness living behind her eyes like a parasite. Ghost eyes. I said to myself: You're lying. She was full of life and confidence and the usual death defiance. Only when she disappeared did she become an omen. She once said: *It's unlikely I'll make it past thirty.* But I'd said that too, as all young people have at some point, one early morning watching the sun rise over the rooftops.

I lifted my hand and pressed my index finger to the steam, drew a circle, and turned to Alba. Across the street was a bar. Over the door hung a pink neon sign. The word TOPLESS blinked against the winter sky. We'd not noticed the sign before, but now it suddenly seemed magnetic. We were drawn to it as if by force, crossed the street without looking. The usual engine sounds were coming from the mountain, but otherwise all was quiet. The snow fell and fell and gathered in drifts. We stood under the neon sign and let it bathe us in its pink glow. I imagined a scene where a large group of men in identical full-dress uniforms threw themselves over a cake. Inside the cake a beautiful girl was kneeling with her eyes closed. They lifted their spoons.

The sign blinked above us, and we flung open the door. The room was thick with tobacco smoke. We sat down at a dark-wood corner table. Between us stood a yellow candle and an ashtray shaped like a star.

A barmaid came over. She was dressed in sequined underpants and high-heeled sandals with rhinestones. Covering each nipple was a metal heart. *What'll it be*, she said. *Liqueur*, Alba said. She took out a cigarette and lit it for me. I arranged my dress over my knee, crossed my legs, and wagged my foot. I smoked my cigarette, sighing loudly between each puff. I stared at the framed postcard hanging above the table where we sat. There were various shellfish laid out on a sparkling silver platter. Here and there some fallen black rose petals. My left cheek sensed that Alba was looking at me. I turned my head and looked at her. She just stared at me without a word.

We were given our liqueurs. We raised our glasses and toasted. I reached out my hand and took out yet another cigarette, leaned into the flame of the candle. The cigarette flared in front of my face, and my chest burned. I looked at the high street, which still lay empty.

Alba said: *Strega, a place for idiots and the dogs of idiots.*

I laughed.

I said, in a murderer's voice: *One could lure away the barmaid. Do things to her. Tie her to a tree or put her in a metal box. Let her lie in the dark for days on end.*

Alba said, in the same voice: *One could burn her. Pour hot liquids over her. One could swaddle her in white sheets, until she can no longer move, until she becomes a doll.*

I turned my gaze to the table. Brought my glass to my mouth and wet my lips. Alba was chain-smoking beside me. Her breathing became more and more labored. We sat like this for hours. I don't know how long. Music was coming out of the speakers. The same record again and again. We waved the barmaid over, ordered by pointing to one bottle after another. We spent all our money on sweet drinks. We toasted like men. We said many terrible things. I took out my lipstick and painted my lips without a mirror. I turned to a woman at the next table, complimented her earrings and rings, asked her name. I heard myself say meaningless lines, which I borrowed from the sleeping parts of my brain. Lines from hospital novels and films.

I took out my notebook and continued working on the list of the various murder victims I'd read about:

Girl murdered in the mountains among other girls.

Girl murdered on the beach, sand in her hands.

Girl murdered next to factory, chemical smoke, setting sun.

Girl murdered under her own sheets.

Girl murdered, unidentified.

Girl murdered, rose hip in mouth.

Girl murdered on her way home.

Girl murdered, tattoo at left eye.

Girl murdered, never buried.

Alba sat across from me and said things like: *Don't forget the one with the razor blades.* Or: *Was it really the left eye.* Her hands were never still. She kept dripping candle wax on her wrists or stacking matchboxes in piles. She rapped her finger in front of me on the table. She said: *If one were to go to the nuns.* I lifted my gaze from the paper and put down my pen. She looked at me with her steady gaze. *Have a look around. The relics and the herbs.* I opened my eyes wide. Said nothing, but nodded.

We downed the liqueur. We stubbed out our cigarettes. We headed for the nuns. Outside the bar, the main street was still empty. We dragged our hands through the thin fog. The air was no longer icy, but it was cold. The frosty nights lined up like a row of black pearls. I stared out into the milky darkness, trying not to vomit. I noticed a flash across the street, something golden and gleaming. I squinted to see what it was. I thought Cassie was whispering something in my ear and shook my head to make her stop. Suddenly, I saw that it was the Ophelia miniature that was gleaming. A shining oval in the dense darkness. I looked at my hands, which had begun to tremble, went over and rested my forehead on Alba. She stroked my hair and said my name.

We headed for the convent. The forest exhaled around us. After Cassie's disappearance, a new rhyme had become popular among the local children. Now we could hear someone singing in the darkness. In my mind's eye I saw them walking past in the mountains, in their shorts and starched collars. They were singing: *One maid walked into the woods, then she was gone. Two maids walked into the woods, then they were gone. Seven maids walked into the woods, then they were gone. Twelve maids walked into the woods, then they were gone. Thirteen maids walked into the woods, then they were gone.*

It was after midnight, and we had been walking for a long time. We had trudged through the snow for hours. The forest had been eerie but also beautiful. Around us the night had grown colder and colder, but we kept walking. We finally stumbled upon the convent, as if by chance. Now it lay before us, hard and closed. There was a scent of olibanum and wax. There was the scent of sage, of cold rock. Everything was covered in frost.

The nuns had gathered for a nightly prayer. Their voices like hard rain on the face: *Have mercy, have mercy! Hear us! Have mercy on us, holy Mary, holy Virgin! Mother, thou mother of grace, thou mother of purity, thou mother without blemish, thou beloved mother, thou virgin. Thou virgin. Thou virgin, thou mirror. Thou chalice, thou precious chalice, thou rose. Thou mysterious rose, thou tower, thou golden house, thou evening star. Thou queen of martyrs. Thou rosary. Thou mirror, thou mirror, thou rose.*

We stood still. I was a pillar in the night. The nuns fell silent, and we heard them getting up. Through a gap in the wall, incense seeped out, heavy and sweet. Alba went over and pressed her ear to the chapel door. She allowed her nail to scrape across the wood. She whistled a high note. I heard someone say: *That's not me, it's someone else.* Something white fluttered in the darkness, and we looked up. Above us, a nun was waving a handkerchief out of a window. She was whistling almost inaudibly. It was a melody I had heard before, a hymn perhaps. It sounded like she wanted to beckon something from the darkness. Alba said: *Come down.* Her voice sounded sharp in the lofty silence. I leaned against the stone wall and shut my eyes. I still felt sick from the booze. I lit two cigarettes and handed one to Alba.

We stood and smoked for a while in silence. Nothing happened. We smoked and kept quiet. We were just about to give up and head back to the Olympic when the nun appeared in the chapel door. She was lit from above by the mad moon. Pressed her finger to her jugular notch, where a gold cross was glittering. She looked like a bride on her way to the wedding ceremonies. Her hair fell heavy over her shoulders and framed an indomitable face. I thought she had Cassie's eyes. The same black globes. The same thick black eyebrows, shaped like half-moons. In her eyes was the trust of innocence and the lunacy of innocence. She had hidden her hair under her wimple, but it was under there, growing, unseen. She took our hands and said her name. In her name was the nun of the coniferous forest, the name of a butterfly, a pest.

She said: *Come.* We followed her across the cloister garth, which was filled with nightly scents, frozen earth and dead plants, the particular scent of cold fabrics. She had nothing in her hands but looked like she was holding a hymnbook or a basket, a wax candle shaped like a saint. We arrived at a building, a kind of storehouse, that lay hidden behind a wall of wintergreen Siberian carpet cypress. The windows were foggy. She ran her hand over the glass and it left a mark. Around us the darkness was blue and all-consuming. She opened the door and opened out her arm, as if to say: *This is my temple.* She went up to a small table in the middle of the room. Lit some candles and an oil lamp. On the table were books and documents, dried flowers and icons, a porcelain bowl with beads and caramels, crucifixes and hymnbooks, empty bottles of perfume. The nun pointed to a low bunk and asked us to sit. She looked at us for a long time in the yellow light, then sat down on a stool in the middle of the room and started talking. Her voice was soft, but somehow mechanical, and I got the idea that she was a machine, crackling away beside me in the night. She said:

Once I was in a place called Marienberg, where I spent a week sleeping on a metal bed, made up with sheets that gave off a chemical smell. On the wall hung the crucifix. It was a large international hotel, colossal and baroque, with an extravagant but somehow dead interior. I walked shoeless through the hotel. This was before the veil, before the ceremonies. The carpeting was soft underfoot. I walked slowly and took it all in. A spiral staircase ran through the building like a damaged spine. Somewhere a child or a baby was crying. I followed the sound awhile, but gave up. Its echo hammered between the floors. One moment the cry was coming from the basement, the next it changed pitch and sounded like a woman moaning. I passed a man going from room to room, through endless corridors, looking for a woman. He said: We met last year. I shook my head, went back to my room. In the bathroom was black wallpaper that shimmered when you turned on the ceiling light. There were hanging urns and climbing plants. There was an enamel bowl, in which yellow rosebuds were floating in cloudy water. I bent down and rinsed my face. When I lifted my gaze, I was looking right into the Madonna's eyes. This was my sign.

I went straight from the hotel to the convent. I wanted to study the madness alive in the language of saints. I wanted it to reveal its precept. A saint can say: He came to me in a different guise, he was a boy who walked on the shoreline, he carried a ball and a cone of caramels, and she is believed. But it quickly became apparent that this is no place for madness, but a place for discipline. You see, a nun's life is a performance that is repeated for an eternity. One does the same thing each day, choreographed.

After a while, the body grows accustomed to falling asleep in the light and waking in the dark. At first one is woken up by one of the others, but after a few weeks the body gets used to it and follows the collective rhythm, the convent clock. It is an order that penetrates the flesh and stays there, until all is order. One is a doll that someone takes apart and puts back together. The mouth smiles as it always has done, but the arms are set the wrong way round, the palms face forward. One becomes a person outside of time. One forgets all one knows about day and night, about the morning, about the afternoon sun. One is a stage on which someone else's life can play out. One makes no experiences.

It is important for you both to understand one thing. Ceremony is this: taking something apart and putting it back together. I went through the ceremony of the veil and the ceremony of the victim. There was a run in my stockings and it felt like an omen. I spoke my own name. The name I'd had as a baby and the name I was to have as a nun. I received the cloth with my hands. My complicated hairstyle was a symbol of the work ahead, my perseverance. The silk ribbon around my head: a symbol of everything else, the forsaken. I went into the room where the abbess was waiting. She pointed to a mirror and said nothing. I walked up to it and saw myself in the wimple. I started crying. I was a moth or something wilted. I was a table with a white cloth. A piece of bread, an aspergillum, a candle one pays for with a small coin.

She fell silent and looked at us, got up slowly. I wanted to say something, but she held up a finger to her mouth. She turned her gaze to the window, as if she could see someone out there. Then started taking out various pungent boxes and jars. She heated something on a camp stove. It crackled and smoked. She lit incense and dipped her hands in holy water. She gave us small rounded glasses to drink from. The liquid was hot and orange and we drank it in small sips. It tasted of hibiscus and medicine. I looked at Alba. Her eyes were misty, and her lips were shiny from the drink.

I lay down on the bunk and closed my eyes. I was sleepy but couldn't sleep. I turned my eyes inward. Inside my eyes I saw various signs. Out of a rock crevice rose a woman's body, covered in fresh green leaves. From the sand on a beach came a woman crawling. Damp marble walls appeared in brief flashes. I saw a bloody girl hanging from the ceiling. I saw blue light with one eye and red with the other. I saw seven faces come floating out of the darkness, illuminated from below by as many votive candles. A woman sat in the tall grass cleaning a pile of bones. I reached out to touch her. I could hear Alba's voice, but as through water. It sounded like a voice speaking from a place beyond death. The body seemed to dissolve and then reassemble itself, in another more mechanical form. The nun's voice was also there. I trusted her even though I probably shouldn't. I sent my hand out for Alba but couldn't reach her. Things appeared and vanished, as if they were subject to a strict discipline, an evil order.

I felt the nun sit down next to me. The scent of holy water and cotton came from her. She took my hand. I felt her stroking my palm with various things. Feathers, silk, knives. It hurt, but I didn't scream. I had always wanted to be a kept woman. To be dressed, fed, beaten. Held tight in a gleaming, oily lead.

Alba's hair swept past my face, and I tried to catch it with my mouth. I opened my eyes and looked at her through the darkness. A scorpion had settled between her eyes like a jewel. Thick smoke rose up from her throat to the ceiling. I looked away and straight into the nun's face, which hung over me, staring. Her eyes turned green and black and green again. I reached out and ran a finger over her cheek, leaving a trail. She smiled. My eyes turned inward again. I saw everything in an electric light. The interior of my body was lit up like a dissection room in a medical school somewhere. Men in white coats walked through the room, pointing at my inner organs with metal objects. Someone paused to say: *Look!*

I fell asleep and slept in fits. Many hours passed. I froze, I sweated. With the dawn the character of the cold changed. I woke to find that I was lying under a dark yellow silk blanket.

I was shivering, but felt wide awake, as if someone had flushed out my brain with holy water. A gray light streamed through the window and over to us. The nun was gone. I got up. My legs were unsteady, but I knew them to be mine. In the middle of the room, the nun had left a mirror. I placed myself in front of it. I knew I was insignificant but beautiful. Behind me I saw the room reflected. On the bed lay locks of hair, feathers, under-pants. The sheet was stained with the orange drink. I looked at myself. A girl whose red eyes are pursuing a bewitched trail. In the mirror, I became a frog, a panther, a lizard with an insect's head. A peppery smell came from my hair. The hands wrapped around each other. My eyes were clear as streams. I recognized them.

I turned around and looked at Alba. She was lying on the floor with her eyes shut. I picked her up and carried her out through the door and on across the cloister garth. I carried her through the woods, wrapped in my winter coat. The mountains were before us, gleaming in the morning light. My hair flowed heavy down my back. It was soaking wet, I couldn't remember why. I looked down at Alba. Her face was calm, but very old. She weighed nothing. I was a statue of the Madonna, carrying her brother through the peaceful morning. At the lake I stopped. I laid her in the moss, splashed her face with water. She woke up and looked at me. Pressed her hand to my forehead. The sun was high above the mountains, like a sun in summer, glowing hot and flame yellow, in the midst of the silent winter. I turned to it and raised my hand in greeting. I looked at Alba. She got up slowly, staring straight ahead, as if she could see someone in the empty air, someone she recognized. I took her hand and held it tight. We headed for the hotel.

We stood side by side and stared down at the pool. There were algae and small fish. There was a red plant climbing the walls. We dove to the bottom, where various things were floating past the pale blue tile. Metal cutlery, swimming goggles, a green candle. A pair of cotton panties had gotten stuck in the drain. In one corner was a brooch that I felt like picking up but let lie because I got it into my head that it was haunted. I swam three lengths without coming up for air, then turned to face that strange sun. The winter sky hung over us, breathing. The pool was filled with a dark green, cloudy water. We were dirty and tried to wash ourselves. Everything hurt. Body and soul and the backside of the soul. I rested my chin on the edge of the pool and looked up at the hotel. It looked like a red insect shimmering in the haze. Rex was watching us from a window. I swam on. As I passed Alba, I whispered: *She's here.*

We stayed in the pool until our fingers grew stiff and our

stomachs felt empty and hollow. We climbed the ladder and crept over to a deck chair. We lay down close together, pulling our dresses over us like blankets. The feel of the plastic against our arms and the aromatic forest. I saw the nun's shining eyes in front of me like a form of proof. We were cold. For a moment we had an urge to stay right where we were and never get up. I could sense Rex watching us. She did nothing. She let us lie.

I said: *Do you think it was her? Do you think it was Cassie?* I shut my eyes, as if afraid of my own question and unwilling to hear the answer. Alba said: *But she was a redhead. But she had the face of a nun.* We lay there for a while, staring up at the sky. The silence was soft, as it always was between us, a beautiful shawl strewn with flowers and jewelry, something velvety to wrap around oneself. We were silent. On my hands were the marks from the nun's nails. The cold had spread from my feet to my knees. I thought my hair was giving off a smell of black mold.

I said: *What do we do now?*

And Alba replied: *We go home.*

☽

We folded paper birds, looked out over the landscape. The world lay there, brittle and rotten. We heard boys singing on the forest path. It was during a thaw. Someone had switched on the fountain. Its gurgling reached all the way up to us. We were feverish and tired and dressed like soldiers. The sun was on its way down behind the mountains and everything was dizzying. When we came into the lobby, dripping with pool water, the warmth felt like grace. We went to the bathroom and rinsed our hands with hot water. We fetched coffee from the kitchen. Costas was at the stove making jam. She looked at us and shook her head, handed us each a chilled orange. And then there we were, sitting on the windowsill, hair wrapped in towels, eating grapes from a bowl.

We had talked for a long time. We had agreed that for many months, the hotel had been launching a sort of two-pronged attack on us. I said: *The evil comes from within and the evil comes from without.* Alba nodded. We were more and more convinced that someone had poisoned the drinking water. It always tasted bitter and seemed to shimmer green when we held the glass up to the kitchen window. All day, we had whispered the same string of words: *We offer up our prayers, our deeds and sacrifices on this day so that we will be able to leave this place. Blame and the distribution of blame.*

In my head, the same thought repeated: What if one could be free? Walk in a different way, through city parks and department stores. I could walk in my yellow dress and not care about a thing. On the ground floor, I could try on a glove, it might fit perfectly, I might let it slip into my pocket. I said out into the room: *I offer up my prayers, my deeds and sacrifices on this day so that I will be able to leave this place. Blame and the distribution of blame.*

I looked down at the paper birds. The hands were working. I looked out the window. Meltwater, roses. As if upon a stage the nun became visible in the curbed, dead landscape. She appeared in her black-and-white robe, carrying a plaited bag with a tourist motif. She passed the hotel, en route to the cable car. I saw her shoes, which gleamed, I saw her face. I turned to Alba and said: *Look.* She said: *If she can go, then so can we.*

)

We were going to leave Strega. We were going to travel through a dead landscape. We were going to catch the scent of ivy and rock. We decided that, before we left the Olympic, we would organize a memorial service for Cassie. A ritual to honor her memory, but also to banish the evil that we suspected would otherwise follow us through our lives and into death.

We raised an altar to her in the middle of the ballroom. Her portrait leaned against a silver candelabra with pink candles. Everywhere the scent of incense and soap. Fabrics we had dipped in her perfume. A lock of her hair. When I stood next to the altar, I could sense her whole being, like a vibrating presence, a phantom. I held out my hands and shut my eyes. In the darkness behind my eyes, her mouth emerged, bright red and smiling. It said: *Rafa*. I opened my eyes.

The nuns turned up, in mourning dress. Roses fastened at the heart or on the arm. We had dispatched Alexa to invite them.

Rex and Costas looked at each other with wide eyes. The nuns had never been inside the walls of the hotel before. They walked right up to Cassie's altar. Pressed their fingers to their lips, pressed their fingers to her forehead, said: *Requiescat in pace.* Then sat down at the table with the biscuits and wine, toasted Cassie with great solemnity.

I looked at Rex. I saw her mask fall away and reveal her interior, something strong and shimmering. She walked over to the abbess and took a seat.

I danced only with Alba that night. Face close to hers. Her scent of rain and sweat. Her hair, redolent of patchouli. Our bodies were suddenly soft, moving through the room in a perfect choreography. The heat of her hands and all that was hot. I held her tight. I knew then that it was over. I knew our friendship was eternal but had a fixed term, that it ended with this night. I leaned forward and bit her neck gently. She smiled. This was our sign.

Night came, and with the night, we walked to the dormitory. We packed our things. We hummed quietly, a melody from the evening. The music was still playing. The night was beautiful but uneasy. Thunder and violets. We held this mourning ball, and when the day dawned, we left the hotel.

We walked through the corridor with our suitcases. The carpeting was dusty in the harsh light. This was no longer our job, we let it be dusty. Our hands felt light, even though what we were carrying was heavy. One wanted to reach them to the ceiling. One wanted to be part of a great formation. One wanted to dance in sync in yellow chiffon as a river flowed through the city, steel gray and still, colored lanterns shining along the quay. We walked through the lobby and let our steps echo. We slammed the door shut, not caring about a thing. We took each other's hands and breathed.

We walked. It was dawn. The steam rose from the earth and kept rising. A cold shine had settled over the mountains, their peaks hidden by pink clouds. The Olympic lay behind us, we did not turn around. Strega was below us, we did not look in that direction. We said nothing. I saw Alba in a particular light. My eyes gulped it down. We were two people on a walk through the mountains. I saw the mountains and the sky, which was thundering. I saw the meltwater and the earth and the slick stones. I saw the rock crystals and the mines and the center of the earth. Magma and obsidian and the fiery red interior of everything.

We had arranged the crime scene before we left. We had made our beds, setting them like a dangerous stage. We wanted them to know we were gone before they knew we were gone. The room was to vibrate with our absence. We would hang from the ceiling like a curse. We would sit in the walls like a bad memory, a stain that emerged from the carpeting each night.

We'd held vigil the whole night through. We'd whispered to each other: *We can only find a way out of this crime scene by constructing one of our own.* We watched the hands tending to their tasks. In front of us, the beds stood in tidy rows. We had each left behind a mark of our own, an amulet of our own. I had laid out my green bracelet. The plastic beads lay on the pillow like a tuft of seaweed. On Alba's pillow lay three dried plants. A small bouquet of rose geranium, water mint, and belladonna. They rustled against the pillowcase, bound with a thick and dirty string. We left everything as we wanted them to find it. We knew that a girl's life could at any point be turned into a crime scene. This was our crime scene.

We walked and walked and evening came. We were tired and walked to a village at the foot of a mountain. We ate bread and meat in a dusky restaurant. We slept close together in a narrow bed. I took in Alba's smell. I knew that this was the last time. I lied when I said: *We'll see each other again soon. We'll live a long life close to each other. We'll build a home together. A small apartment, maybe, with a balcony and yellow walls. The face of a building thick with plants. And every morning, we'll wake up together, and the day will lie before us like a happy thing.*

)

I woke up early and went to wash my face with cold water and soap. Through the window, I saw the sun rising over the mountains like I don't know what, a beautiful orb. I stood like that until everything was bathed in the same light. I turned to the sink. In the mirror, I recognized the death that is in the eyes of those who have been awake since sunrise. Those who have seen the night retreat and the morning spill forth.

I woke Alba, running my hand over her cheek, whispering her name. She opened her eyes, and we looked at each other. We went down to the dining room. It was a brown room with no panels. We drank milk and ate black bread with honey. We said nothing. We got up and pushed in our chairs. At the door, we nodded to the innkeeper, took her hand. We walked. Through the forest, the mountains, past lakes, streams, rivulets. We walked and walked, and the silence grew heavier and heavier, but we carried it like something holy.

At a fork in the road, we parted. We didn't say much to each other. I kissed her on the mouth. We stood like that for a long time. The ground disappeared beneath us, and we sank through the strata of earth. We looked at each other. Whispered: *My friend, my beloved.* We looked at each other, nodded, backed away from each other, like two youths in an armed duel, an impossible dawn where the dew lies heavy over the courtyard, the palace garden draped in glass and fabric, a celebration that has fallen through the air and landed.

I walked. By lakeside villas with the lights off and cemeteries and alpine fields. Many days went by. I passed small villages and communities, but not a single city. I bought bread from a woman and ate it. The mountains seemed endless. Gold moons followed crystal moons. I slept under the open sky. There came nine bright and wet days. On the tenth day, I arrived in a town with a railway station. I bought a ticket. I climbed on board.

)

I went back once, as an adult. It was in the spring. I was thirty
years old. I'd brought my child with me. He walked beside me
and held my hand. It was a hot day, and we were sweating. I had
dressed him in his long cotton shirt. On his feet he wore rubber
sandals. When we arrived with the train, we had to sit down at a
bar next to the station. The heat and silence were stupefying. I
ordered a glass of iced tea for me and a bottle of lemon soda for
him. We drank and looked at each other across the table. He was
quiet but seemed happy. He got up to take a lap around the
square. The time on the clock inside the station building was
still wrong. I lit a cigarette. I saw him stop by a tree and pick
something up off the ground. I saw that he was struggling in the
heat. His shirt had wet patches, and his hair had curled at the
neck. I called him over, plucked an ice cube from my glass, and
ran it across his forehead. I buried my nose in his hair. He held
out his hand and showed me what he had found, a perfectly

round stone. We walked to the cable car. I held his hand, we sweated. We waited a long time. The timetable showed that it only ran a couple of times a day. There were almost no people around. The sun burned our faces. I dug out a handkerchief from my bag and tied it around his head. The cable car arrived, and we climbed aboard. He held his ticket in his hand. We traveled between the mountains. Below us lay the valley. The contours blurred in the heat and the sun was high. I dug out a piece of soft, spongy bread and handed it to him. He ate looking out over the mountains. We arrived and got off. I took his hand. The air was thinner here, but it was cooler. There was a pressure in my chest. I could hear my child's lungs working. I wanted to move into his body and breathe for him. His sandals were dusty. We walked along the stone wall through the forest. I had forgotten this mad silence and the smells. A bird sounded, and we looked up. There were paper decorations hanging from the trees. I squeezed his hand. We cooled our cheeks against the wall. We breathed heavily. We walked on. I avoided looking into the forest. The gates appeared before us. The child pointed, and I nodded. Dust flew around us. He bent down and picked up some earth. I pushed open the gates with my foot. The hotel lay empty. The facade had faded even more and was almost light pink. Everything was in decay except the park, which was well maintained. The bushes were trimmed, and the flowers were healthy in their beds below the kitchen windows. There was a smell of cold water and chlorophyll. The entrance was open. My child had found a shovel and was digging in the gravel over by the fountain. I waved. He smiled. I went in and lingered there breathing for a while. In the lobby, no time had passed. The phone was still on the wall. The guest book lay open on the reception desk. There was a thick film of dust everywhere. I ran my hand over the wall of mirrors, on which a photograph was taped. A picture of us, lined up along the facade. Alba's young face. My child cried out, and I flinched. My pulse was racing. I ran into the courtyard. He was sitting by the fountain. It was glistening. He was holding something in his hands.